Mystery of the Silver Coins

Other Titles by Lois Walfrid Johnson

Viking Quest

1. *Raiders from the Sea*
2. *Mystery of the Silver Coins*
3. *The Invisible Friend*
4. *Heart of Courage*
5. *The Raider's Promise*

Series also available in Norwegian

The Freedom Seekers

1. *Escape into the Night*
2. *Race for Freedom*
3. *Midnight Rescue*
4. *The Swindler's Treasure*
5. *Mysterious Signal*
6. *The Fiddler's Secret*

Adventures of the Northwoods

1. *The Disappearing Stranger*
2. *The Hidden Message*
3. *The Creeping Shadows*
4. *The Vanishing Footprints*
5. *Trouble at Wild River*
6. *The Mysterious Hideaway*
7. *Grandpa's Stolen Treasure*
8. *The Runaway Clown*
9. *Mystery of the Missing Map*
10. *Disaster on Windy Hill*

Series also available in German and Swedish

Faith Girlz: Girl Talk: 52 Weekly Devotions

Also available in in the UK

For adults: Either Way, I Win: God's Hope for Difficult Times

MYSTERY of the SILVER COINS

LOIS WALFRID JOHNSON

MOODY PUBLISHERS
CHICAGO

Glendalough is a real place—an Irish monastery that grew from the inspiration of St. Kevin in the 6th century. I've described Glendalough as it was in the late 900's. But with the exception of St. Kevin and St. Patrick, all names and characters, including Brother Cronan, Bree, Devin, their family, and friends are fictitious.

Brynjulf, a high-ranking chieftain, and his son are described in Egil's saga and *Among the Fjords and Mountains: A Summary of Aurland's History,* as living in Aurland, Norway, before the year 900. With the exception of Brynjulf and his son, who are mentioned in the acknowledgments, not the story, all names and characters, including Mikkel, his family, and friends are fictitious.

Any resemblance to persons living or dead is coincidental.

The prayer in chapter 8 is from the *Book of Cerne,* tenth century, and in public domain. From *A Celtic Psaltery,* compiled by David Adam, London: SPCK, 2001.

Published in association with the literary agency of Alive Communications, Inc., 7680 Goddard Street, Suite 200, Colorado Springs, Colorado 80920.

Cover Design: Barb Fisher, LeVan Fisher Design
Text Illustrations: Greg Call
Interior Design: Ragont Design
Editor: Cessandra Dillon

ISBN: 978-0-8024-3113-4

Printed by Bethany Press International in Bloomington, MN – 3/2019

We hope you enjoy this book from Moody Publishers. Our goal is to provide high-quality, thought-provoking books and products that connect truth to your real needs and challenges. For more information on other books and products written and produced from a biblical perspective, go to www.moodypublishers.com or write to:

Moody Publishers
820 N. LaSalle Boulevard
Chicago, IL 60610

9 10

Printed in the United States of America

To Anders Ohnstad
because you have chosen to live with courage
and to
each of you
who choose to do the same

CONTENTS

INTRODUCTION

Today Bergen, Norway is known as the only city in the world surrounded by seven mountains and seven fjords. It is believed that during Viking times there was a small settlement called Holmen in the area where King Haakon's Hall and the Rosenkrantz Tower now stand. It is also believed that a king's farm named Alrekstad was located nearby.

If you're in Bergen and would like to see this story through the eyes of Bree, Mikkel, and their friends, climb the trails or take the cable railway up Mount Fløyen. Enjoy the view and the fun of knowing that there could be a mystery right under your feet!

ONE

ESCAPE!

In the silence of night Briana O'Toole's deep brown eyes peered into the darkness. As she waited for exactly the right moment, the wind off the Norwegian Sea caught her flyaway hair. On the Viking ship around her other prisoners slept, but Bree kept watch. This might be her one hope of escape.

A few hours earlier, Vikings had drawn their longship onto a beach on the west coast of Norway. Now the two men standing guard on one side of the ship began talking to guards on the other side. And still Bree waited.

On that September night late in the tenth century, time grew long. Then came the moment Bree hoped for.

When a black cloud moved above the ship, the heavens opened, and rain poured down upon them.

At the far end of the ship the four guards took refuge under the sail spread out like a tent. Without making a sound, Bree woke her young friend Lil.

"Shhh! Don't speak!" Bree whispered close to her ear. "It's time to go."

Silently they dropped their bundles from the ship. As they climbed over the side, the full force of the storm struck them. Wind and rain slashed at Bree's face as she snatched up the bundles she had prepared. Giving one to Lil, Bree took the rest herself and started across the beach.

Pounding rain covered the sound of their feet on the small stones near the shore. In the dark of the storm no moon betrayed them. No stars gave them light. Staying as far as possible from other ships in the harbor, Bree headed for a line of trees behind a cluster of houses.

When they reached the trees, Bree pulled Lil into the shadows and stopped to listen. In that instant a dog barked.

Lil gasped. Reaching out, Bree touched her arm in warning. As still as the stones of the land they stood.

The bark came from a house close to the shore. In spite of the rain, Bree could see the dark outline of the back of the house. If the dog startled the guards on Mikkel's ship—if the guards found prisoners missing—if they went to find Mikkel—

If, if, if. All of them held the threat of danger. And all of them centered on Mikkel.

Only one year older than Bree, the fourteen-year-old led the band of Vikings that had captured the two girls. When the raiders plundered a monastery in the Wicklow Mountains of Ireland, they carried off rich treasure. From the surrounding countryside they took captives for ransom or slavery.

Again the dog barked. If the guards knew something was wrong, they would bring Mikkel back to the ship. As his prisoners, Bree and Lil were now slaves. That is, unless they escaped.

The next time the dog barked, it sounded closer. As though in reply, a second dog barked, then a third.

Lil shivered in fear. "Can we climb a tree?" she whispered.

Bree looked up. The lowest branches were far above them. Even if she lifted Lil on her shoulders, the younger girl wouldn't be able to reach.

As the pounding rain changed to a soft mist, a dog rounded the corner of the house. Even in the dark, Bree could see its white hair. Head to the ground, it sniffed its way along the side wall.

Moments later another dog joined the first. Yipping between themselves, they moved back and forth, close to where Bree and Lil had walked.

Bree held her breath. Did the rain wash away our scent?

Kneeling down behind a tree, Bree opened one of her bundles. Deep inside was the small hoard of food she had hidden away. If the dogs found them, she needed to be ready.

Her hands cold with fear, Bree touched the pieces of flatbread. If she gave them to the dogs, she and Lil would have no food. Filled with dread, Bree started to pray.

In ever-widening circles the dogs moved out, their noses to the ground. Then a third dog joined the first two. How many *are* there? An entire pack?

Yipping and barking, the dogs came closer and closer to where Bree and Lil hid.

"Don't let them see you're afraid," Bree whispered. But her own heart thumped. Were Viking dogs as fierce as their owners?

Once again she touched the food inside her bundle. At the same time she felt it was hopeless. How could she ever make friends by giving the dogs a few pieces of flatbread?

As the minutes stretched long, Bree heard a woman call to the dogs. Holding a candle, she, too, came around the corner of the house. With her hand cupping the flame, she protected it from wind and rain. When the light reflected in her face, Bree saw flaming red hair.

For an instant the woman glanced toward the line of

trees behind her house. Then a small boy followed her into the backyard. "What's wrong, Mamma?" he asked.

"Nothing." The woman's voice carried clearly, as though she purposely spoke louder than needed. But the dogs kept sniffing the ground. Though they hadn't found a trail, they drew closer and closer to Bree and Lil.

Without moving the woman stared at the trees, as though seeing between them. In the light of the candle Bree saw her look toward the place where she and Lil hid.

"What's wrong, Mamma?" the boy asked again.

"Everything is all right," she told him, then called the dogs. With a last *yip* they went to her.

Reaching down, the woman took the boy's hand. "Come," she said. "Back to bed with you."

With the three dogs trailing behind, the woman walked toward the front of the house. Just before passing out of sight, she turned. Again she looked straight toward where Bree and Lil hid.

Weak with relief, Bree stood there, hardly able to believe they had been spared. Retying her bundle, she slung it over her shoulder. With a second bundle under her other arm, she was ready to move on. But Bree forced herself to wait.

As the rain started again, pounding down upon the earth, the spreading branches of oak and birch trees sheltered them from the worst of the storm. From farther away came the crash of waves washing against the shore.

But Bree knew that without the light of moon or stars she could lose her direction. She could even walk in a circle back to Mikkel's ship.

In stillness unbroken by dogs or people, Bree thought about the lay of the land. In the last light of day she had looked up to the mountains surrounding the Norwegian harbor. Farther inland, beyond the peninsula where Mikkel's ship was drawn up on shore, the ground slanted gradually upward, then rose in steep slopes.

Now Bree decided that if she and Lil headed that way, then kept walking uphill, they wouldn't lose their sense of direction. Though they didn't know where they were going, they would be moving away from Mikkel and his ship.

"Stay as close to me as you can," Bree whispered in Lil's ear.

At first the ground was flat and open, then it changed so gradually that Bree needed to keep thinking about the slope beneath her feet. Dodging low branches, she made her way between trees. *Dawn,* Bree reminded herself. By dawn they had to be hidden away. When the sun rose, Mikkel would discover that they were missing.

Already, the young Viking had the broad shoulders and strong body of a boy used to hard work. Lured by the riches that pilgrims brought to the monastery near Bree's home, Mikkel had gone ahead of his men to explore the Wicklow Mountains. When Bree first saw him, she thought he was Tully, a friend of her family. Then, while crossing a river, Mikkel fell and hit his head on a stone.

Bree still felt that moment of terror. Without knowing who he was, she had saved Mikkel's life. Soon after, he led his band of Vikings into the peaceful Irish countryside. Vikings took Bree, Lil, and other prisoners away on their ship.

On their dragon. In the voyage between Ireland and Norway Bree often looked up at the fierce dragon head at the bow of their ship. She had not grown used to its snarling mouth. She knew only that the longship took her away from her family forever. That is, unless Bree escaped, and Lil with her.

Escape they would. Bree would make sure of that.

Though eight years old, Lil's small, thin body made her seem younger. While she had dark blue eyes and black hair, Bree's hair was reddish blond and her eyes deep brown. When morning came, the color of their eyes and hair would add to their danger.

As the ground grew steeper, Bree realized that Lil was panting hard. In spite of their need to hurry, Bree stopped. "We'll rest a minute," she said. "Take long, deep breaths."

When they moved on, Bree took Lil's bundle and set a good pace. Her wet clothing clung to her, but Bree's thoughts raced ahead of her feet. *Dawn,* she told herself again. By dawn at the latest, Mikkel and his men would begin looking for them. And Mikkel would search until he found them.

One thought kept coming back to Bree. *Where can we hide?*

The ground rose sharply upward now. As thick clouds broke apart, the rain stopped, giving enough light so that Bree didn't stumble over rocks. At first she climbed straight up, finding a way wherever she could. Before long, she realized that Lil still struggled to keep up with her.

In spite of her need to hurry, Bree slowed down. With all her heart she wanted to get as far as possible from Mikkel and the harbor. At home Bree was used to climbing the mountain behind her family's farm. But now a knot of fear clutched her stomach. That fear went beyond barking dogs and Mikkel coming after them. Not only did Bree hold her own life in her hands, she needed to take care of Lil.

For more than a week Bree had thought of nothing but escape. They had managed to get away, but now Bree wondered, *Where on this mountain can we be safe?*

Inside, Bree felt a knot of fear. As it moved up into her chest, she felt overwhelmed. In the midst of her panic she started to pray. "Oh, God, please help me. I'm so scared. I can't do this without You."

Moments later, like a whisper on the night wind, Bree heard it. *Don't be afraid. I am with you.*

Bree stopped so suddenly that Lil bumped into her.

I am with you always.

Tears welled up in Bree's eyes. If the Lord was with them, she could go on.

As she and Lil stood there, the last of the clouds moved on and a full moon shone high above the trees. Sifting down between the branches, the moon gave the light they needed. For the first time Bree felt she could see where they were going.

When they set out again, Bree no longer tried to climb straight up the mountain. Instead she walked at an upward slant, turned, and walked back at a higher level. With each step she took, Bree watched and listened.

Born in the mountains of Ireland, she was so used to hearing waterfalls that she nearly missed the ripple of running water. But when she heard it, Bree followed the sound to a narrow stream that fell from one rock ledge to the next.

"You first," Lil whispered, and Bree knelt on the ground. With all the rain the stream was running well. Bree put her hand beneath it, let the water wash over her palm, then drank.

The water was cold, and Bree splashed it over her face. For nearly twenty-four hours she had gone without sleep, but the water brought her alive. As Lil drank deeply, Bree's thoughts hurried on.

"We need a hiding place close by," she whispered.

When they first escaped, the pounding rain had washed away their footprints. But now Bree watched each step that she took. Avoiding soft ground, she stayed on rock, grass, or fallen leaves. Lil followed close behind.

Bree knew exactly what she wanted. A hiding place far enough from the water so that whoever stopped there would not find them. A place that kept them warm and dry. And most of all, a place that hid them.

Searching for such a spot made Bree lonesome for her fourteen-year-old brother, Devin. In the mountains of Ireland they had built a shelter in a cluster of pines. Now Bree tried to find something similar but couldn't. And she and Lil were running out of time.

As the first light of dawn stole across the horizon Bree spotted a boulder a safe distance above the stream of water. An oak tree grew behind and to one side of the large rock. A second oak and a cluster of hazel trees stood nearby.

Bree motioned to Lil. Instead of climbing straight up, they circled around, avoiding soft earth, and keeping to firm ground. Climbing down from above, they stayed on rock ledges and left no footprints.

When they drew close to the boulder, Bree found the hiding place even better than she had hoped. From below she had seen only one large rock. From above, she found rocks around the upper side of a small hollow. The oaks grew close enough to spread their branches like sheltering arms. Bree and Lil climbed the rest of the way down and crawled into their new home.

In the hollow beneath the trees, Lil spread out her reindeer hide blanket. Bree pushed her bundles into spaces between the rocks. Deep beneath the trees, they found a dry spot and stretched out the sealskin tunics they wore over their dresses.

Bree spread her own reindeer hide between Lil and the opening into their hideaway. As Bree snuggled deep beneath her blanket, she remembered she had been up all night.

Yawning, Bree told herself she had to keep watch. Instead, she yawned again and wondered how she could possibly stay awake. She had time for only one prayer. "Father, hide us from their searching eyes."

A moment later, the great distance between Norway and Ireland seemed to be gone, for Bree drifted off to sleep.

TWO

When Mikkel woke just after dawn, he pushed his thatch of blond hair out of his blue eyes and looked around. Tall for his age and with skin bronzed by the sun and wind, he felt like what he was—the master of a Viking longship.

Soon after Mikkel turned fourteen, his father had put him in charge of a merchant ship that sailed from Norway to Ireland. Now the good meal Mikkel devoured the night before still filled his insides. The sealskin bag in which he slept had kept him warm and dry. Best of all, he was back in Norway.

Not only had he traded skins and furs in Dublin, he had raided the Irish countryside, stealing precious gems and other treasures. He had even captured valuable prisoners.

Mikkel grinned. This, the first voyage he'd led, had been successful in every way. How could life be better than that?

What's more, he would return home with his sea chest filled with treasure. Chief among them was a bag of silver coins Mikkel had managed to collect.

Collect? Well, that wasn't quite the word. It wasn't what his father would call it, but for now it would do.

At the thought of his father, Mikkel pushed aside his uneasiness. No time for such gloom today. Instead, he gloated. *After only one trip, I am wealthy!*

Yes, life was good, and soon he would tell all those in his hometown of Aurland how well he had done. From this time on, his fame would grow. In the great halls of the North his name would pass from one storyteller to the next. *Mikkel, son of Sigurd, mighty chieftain of Aurland!* All would know of his brave deeds, his successful voyages, and his great wealth.

But now from the fire and cooking pot on the shore came the scent of food. Freshly caught fish, Mikkel felt sure.

Eager to begin the day, he slipped out of the sealskin bag. His sea chest with its strong iron fittings stood along the side of the ship. Taking a key from the chain on his belt, Mikkel opened the padlock.

Already wearing long, narrow trousers, he found leather bindings and wrapped them around the lower part of his legs. From the chest he took a tunic, a loose garment that fit over his shirt. To that he added his best cloak. Then as Mikkel started to set down his rolled-up bag for sleeping, he looked into the chest.

On the trip to and from Ireland he had eaten most of his flatbread, cheese, and dried cod. Even so, there still was enough to last the rest of the way home. There was also an extra cloak and change of clothes in case he got wet. But suddenly Mikkel knelt down and began moving everything in his chest.

Every piece of clothing was there—every packet of flatbread, cheese, and dried fish. And then he knew. His bag of silver coins was gone.

Mikkel blinked. Rubbing his eyes, he stared at the inside of his sea chest. *Am I dreaming? I have to be wrong.*

Once again he lifted each sealskin, every piece of clothing, even the smallest packages of food. *It's not here!*

Trying to hold back his panic, Mikkel searched yet another time. Finally he could no longer hope that he was imagining things. His stomach churned.

It was here yesterday! It was the last thing I saw last night—

Even to himself, Mikkel did not want to finish the sentence. But the thought pounded away at his mind. The bag of coins was the last thing he had seen before locking the chest and leaving the ship to visit a friend.

Mikkel felt for his knife, still in a sheath on his belt. From the deck of his ship, next to where he slept, he snatched up his sword and thrust it into a second sheath. With one leap he was over the side of the ship and standing before the prisoners who warmed themselves around a fire.

"Take them on board," Mikkel ordered his men.

Mikkel himself had rounded up some of the captives during his raid of the Irish countryside. Now he saw the fear in their eyes. Just as quickly, they looked down at the ground and dragged themselves back onto the Viking ship.

"Line up!" Mikkel's angry voice rang out.

Around the inner sides of the boat the prisoners fell into long rows. Some stood with shoulders back and heads up, unable to hide their anger. Others waited quietly, their gaze off somewhere in the mountains that ringed the harbor. Still others stood with shoulders slumped and heads bowed as they stared down at the deck.

Mikkel picked out four men from the Vikings surrounding the prisoners or standing on the beach outside the ship. All four had stood guard the night before. "My bag of silver coins is missing," Mikkel said.

A murmur passed from one Viking to the next. According to their law, a thief could be punished with death.

"Search the slaves!" Mikkel commanded.

Two by two the guards worked, going down the lines

of prisoners. When the Vikings finished their search, no one could deny the evidence. Not one prisoner had managed to hide even a few coins. If they had once carried some money, it had been taken from them when they were captured.

But Mikkel would not give up so easily. "Search their belongings, and search well."

It took little time to go through the few belongings owned by the prisoners. Again the search turned up nothing. When they finished, the four guards stood next to the prisoners, facing Mikkel.

"So what do you have to say for yourselves? This happened on your watch."

Alf, the shortest guard, as well as the shortest of all the Vikings, stood nearby. In spite of weeks in the wind and sun, the skin of his face looked soft. When he pushed back his knitted cap it stood up in a point. Wisps of light brown hair popped out around his ears.

"It's the trolls," Alf said, his voice filled with dread. "I never thought I'd really see the trolls at work."

"The trolls?" Mikkel tried to show his scorn. Trolls were known for their long crooked noses, ugly faces, and the trouble they brought. Yet Mikkel didn't want to seem afraid.

"They came out of the mountains last night." With a round, smiling face, Alf always seemed more cheerful than the other Vikings. But now he looked uneasy. As though afraid he'd spy a troll, his eyes shifted from one corner of the ship to the other.

As he looked over his shoulder, Alf's soft voice grew even more quiet. "If the trolls took your coins, how can we ever find them?"

Impatient now, Mikkel sighed. "How could it possibly be a troll?" Yet Alf's words started Mikkel thinking. In spite of himself, he glanced toward the mountains. Everyone knew that trolls were so tall that their heads reached above the trees. That's why they lived inside mountains, and that's where they hid their gold and silver.

Mikkel didn't want to get on the wrong side of trolls. They could bring all kinds of trouble into his life.

But the tallest Viking laughed. "Trolls!" he scoffed. Long and lean, Gunnar stood next to Alf. A scruffy beard filled Gunnar's thin face and reached up into the hollows of his cheeks. "You can't blame everything on trolls!"

"Shhhh!" Alf held up his hands to quiet Gunnar. "You'll upset them!"

"That's nonsense!" Gunnar turned to the prisoners. "Who on this longship took the bag of silver coins?"

At Gunnar's words Mikkel turned back to the prisoners. These were the people that he and his men had stolen away from the Irish countryside. Mikkel's gaze traveled from one man, woman, or child to the next. With each passing moment, Mikkel's anger grew. Without doubt he knew who was missing.

"Where is she?" Mikkel asked.

"Where is who?" someone asked. But not one prisoner met his eyes.

"Bree." Mikkel spoke her name as if she were the most despised person on earth. Every prisoner and every Viking knew her name as well as Mikkel. And every person on board ship knew who was missing.

"The girl Bree," Mikkel spit out.

Again a low hum passed between the Vikings. Mikkel acted as if he didn't hear them.

When not a single Irish prisoner answered, Mikkel began counting. Not only was Bree gone, but also one other. Mikkel had watched Bree enough to know who it was. "The girl Bree helps," he said. "What is her name?"

Again, no prisoner met Mikkel's eyes. Every one of them stared at the wood boards of the deck.

"Where did they go?" Mikkel asked. He spoke in Norse, a language used by traders. Though the Irish spoke Gaelic, Mikkel felt sure that some of them also knew Norse. But no one answered his question.

Mikkel waited. "If you do not tell me, their punishment will be upon your heads."

Still no one spoke. Like the stone walls that filled their countryside, the Irish stood together. Mikkel had no doubt they had agreed on what to do.

His steps quick and angry, Mikkel marched over to the first prisoner, lifted his chin, and waited for the

Irishman to look into his eyes. But the prisoner remained silent.

Mikkel did the same with a second, third, and fourth prisoner. Always Mikkel waited until that person returned his gaze. Whether man, woman, boy, or girl, not one Irish captive spoke. Not one of them hinted, even by the look in their eyes, that they knew what had happened to Bree.

Finally Mikkel stepped back. His glance swept up and down the deck, this time taking in each one of the Vikings. To a man, they looked off to sea or the mountains. To a man, they did not meet his gaze. Except for Hauk.

With his gray white hair, flowing beard, and beaklike nose, Hauk resembled a bird of prey. An old hand at sailing, Hauk had worked hard to teach Mikkel everything he knew. But when Hauk became sick, Mikkel made plans of his own. Against everything his father wanted him to do, Mikkel led his men on a raid of the Irish monastery at Glendalough (pronounced Glen da loch).

Now from beneath bushy eyebrows, Hauk's piercing eyes watched Mikkel. And there was something Mikkel knew: This man sent by his father to help him lead the band of Vikings wanted to see how Mikkel met this test.

Mikkel would not disappoint him. His gaze returned to the four guards and lingered on them. "You allowed the captives to escape. What do you have to say?"

"The younger girl is Lil," Alf answered. "But the trolls stole the coins."

Tall, lean Gunnar shook his head. "Trolls!" he scoffed again. "You can't blame everything on them. Bree took the coins."

"Yes, yes," the two other guards chimed in.

"But how?" Mikkel asked. "My sea chest was locked. The key was with me."

"She's a clever one, that girl is." Gunnar seemed eager to explain. "When the night was dark—when we stood outside in the rain—" As if that explained everything, he shrugged.

"So. You did not see her go over the side of the boat?"

"The sail was down, tied to the oar holes."

Mikkel's anger flared. He himself knew how easy it would be to slip out from under the sail at either end of the ship. But he wasn't going to remind all the other prisoners what they could try for themselves.

"There will be no next time," Mikkel told the Vikings. "If any other prisoner escapes, you lose all that you gained in Ireland. And for you four who stood guard so well—" Mikkel's scorn curled around the words. "For you who could not keep two weak-kneed Irish girls as prisoners—you will receive no wages from this trip. No earnings from the furs and goods we sold in Dublin."

For an instant Mikkel's gaze flicked toward Hauk.

When the man nodded, Mikkel knew Hauk was pleased with his decision.

Mikkel looked back to the four guards. Like a smoldering fire, anger burned in the eyes of three of them. Only Alf still seemed convinced that the trolls had made a nighttime visit. Mikkel felt glad. Angry men would not miss an opportunity to find Bree and bring her back.

"That is," Mikkel added, "you lose your wages unless you do one thing. Two Irish lasses should not be difficult to find and capture again."

Mikkel's glance took in the rest of the Vikings. "Now," he ordered, "bind up the prisoners again. When they are tied to the ship, a third of you stay here. The rest of you spread out and find the two girls. Double wages to the man or men who bring them back."

As Mikkel watched, his men tied the wrists of the prisoners. Next they tied a rope around their ankles, leaving only a short length of line between their feet. Then, using a longer rope, they tied each prisoner to the side of the ship. As the Vikings worked, Mikkel studied the four guards.

Gunnar seemed only too glad to search for the girls. The cruel light in his eyes warned Mikkel, sending a chill down his spine.

"Stop!" he ordered, as Vikings started leaving the ship. "Hear this, and hear it well. If either girl is harmed in any way, you will not receive your reward."

With shoulders back and sword in hand, Mikkel waited to be sure each man understood his orders. As he turned from one Viking to the next, each of his men met Mikkel's gaze. But Gunnar looked away.

Unwilling to change his expression by even the flicker of an eyelash, Mikkel waited. "Understood?" he asked again. When Gunnar finally met his gaze and nodded, Mikkel allowed his men to return to breakfast.

The prisoners looked relieved. So, too, did many of the guards. But Mikkel held no doubt about how cruel some of the men could be.

Always Mikkel had been proud of the merchant ship his father built for him. Always Mikkel felt proud that his father sent him out in charge of so many men. But now Mikkel wondered if he could really handle all that was expected of him.

The thought lasted only a moment, for Mikkel had his own answer. *Of course I can. Didn't I earn that bag of silver coins? Didn't I add to all I earned?*

Once again anger flooded his being. *Bree will pay for what she's done.*

But then as Gunnar crossed the deck, Mikkel again saw his eyes. Like a stranger knocking at his door, a thought entered Mikkel's mind. *What did I set loose?*

For the first time in his life Mikkel hated himself. He alone was responsible for the raid on the Glendalough monastery. Only now did he begin to guess at all that his greed had set in motion.

Like another stranger, a warning licked through Mikkel's veins. *If I want to be sure Bree and Lil are safe—*

Mikkel didn't want to finish the sentence, not even to himself. He had only one thought. *I must be the one who finds Bree first.*

THREE

TALE OF THE TWO SISTERS

Deep in the forests of northern Ireland, Devin O'Toole thought about his sister Bree. If only he could know what was happening to her. If only there was some way he could rescue her from the cruel Vikings.

Slender and tall for his age, fourteen-year-old Devin stood straight as an arrow and had their father's black hair and deep blue eyes. A year older than Bree, he had always watched out for her.

He, too, had been stolen away by the Vikings who raided the Irish countryside. When Bree demanded that Mikkel set her brother free, Devin did not want to leave. "You go, instead of me," he told Bree.

But Mikkel gave him no choice. "Go now or not at all!"

And Bree warned, "Do you want Mam and Daddy to lose both of us?"

Sure that he'd still find a way to free his sister, Devin raced up the steep hill next to a sandy beach in northern Ireland. Soon after, Mikkel hurried both prisoners and Vikings on board. As Devin watched, the ship disappeared across the Irish Sea. Each time he thought about it, he felt the pain of losing Bree.

From the top of Ireland, Devin and his ten-year-old friend Jeremy set out for their homes in the Wicklow Mountains south of Dublin. Like Devin, Jeremy had also escaped from the Vikings. Now, long days and nights later, they walked on a road that passed through one of the Glens of Antrim. As the forest surrounded them, the trees crowded close.

Just then Devin heard the footsteps of someone running on the road behind them. When Devin looked back, he saw no one. *But beyond the curve in the road?*

Forcing himself to remain still, Devin listened. By now he had grown used to hearing Jeremy run. His steps were light and quick—the footsteps of a young boy. But these were the steps of someone older and heavier. The steps of a grown man who was coming fast.

Devin leaped up. "Hide!" he told Jeremy, and the boy fled. Devin was right behind him.

Like scared rabbits, they raced into the woods. As the

footsteps drew close, Devin slipped behind the trunk of a large tree and looked back.

Just then the man passed on the road. His hair was blond. He wore a red shirt. And he ran as if he could keep on forever.

Devin groaned. Who was this man? Why was he running as though trying to catch up?

Devin had seen such a shirt on someone hiding in the bushes the day after Mikkel left Ireland. Since then, Devin had wondered if Mikkel left one of his men behind. A man left behind would be angry. An angry man would strike out, trying to get even.

When he and Jeremy started walking again, Devin tried to make light of it. "Whoever that man is, at least he's ahead of us. He's going so fast, we'll never see him again."

Deep inside, Devin wondered about the brave sound of his own words. Without doubt, a man who was angry could make life hard for them.

But Jeremy grinned. With sandy-colored hair and brown eyes, he had a dusting of freckles across his nose. Now he told Devin, "That's blarney, and you know it. It's like saying my freckles make me handsome."

Devin grinned back. Jeremy kept him truthful, all right. When Devin had gone too long without food and water, Jeremy had rescued him. The two boys had been friends ever since.

Pushing his worry aside, Devin looked for berries along the road. On that September day even the rose hips were gone, no doubt eaten by those who passed by.

As the day wore on, Devin's stomach kept rumbling with hunger. For Devin that wasn't unusual, but one thing made it difficult. He and Jeremy were still many miles from the Wicklow Mountains and home.

When the skies opened, drenching them with rain, they kept walking in wet clothes. Devin turned to Jeremy. "Well, lad, Mother O'Leary is at long last washing her floor."

Jeremy grinned. "Sad to say, her goat kicked over buckets of water." But by the end of another hour both of them were so miserable that nothing seemed funny. The more tired Devin became, the more his anger grew. And with it, his hatred for every Viking on earth.

By late afternoon, the boys were walking along a well-traveled road. As Devin looked ahead, he saw a man standing on the side of the road. When he and Jeremy would have passed him by, the man motioned for them to stop.

"Weary you be," he said. "My good master has a place for you."

Careful now about who he trusted, Devin studied the man's face. Already Devin and Jeremy had spent the night sleeping outside in order to be safe. Devin didn't want to be taken in by the wrong person. "A place for us?"

"Aye. A *breen*—a public house that opens its doors to everyone. Don't you know of them, lad?"

Looking around, Devin saw that they stood near a crossroads. Five other roads led to this place. On each road there stood a man guiding people toward a large house.

Thinking back, Devin tried to remember. Hadn't his dad talked of such places all over Ireland?

"It's a place of refuge," Jeremy said.

"For those who have done wrong?"

Jeremy nodded. "If they need a place to flee."

But the man interrupted. "It's also for those who have done right. Be you hungry, lads? Thirsty? My master will take care of you."

"It's free," Jeremy whispered.

Then Devin remembered. Part of the Irish way it was. Hadn't his own mam and dad always taken people in? But here at the crossing of six roads, so many people passed by that there needed to be a man well stocked with animals and servants. A rich man who had at least a hundred of every kind of cattle in his pasture, and a hundred servants as well.

Devin felt relieved. This night he and Jeremy would have a warm place to sleep. Even with appetites as big as the Irish Sea, they would have plenty to eat. And they would be safe. That's what Devin wanted most of all—to be well-fed and safe.

As they passed into a great hall, a long, open fire in

the center of the room took off the chill. Here, where there was plenty of wood to burn, the logs crackled. The smoke escaped through a hole in the roof.

Low tables and benches stretched out on both sides of the fire. Chess players bent over their boards, and men dressed as entertainers sat nearby. Farther away from the fire were the learned men and those with clothing that marked their position in life.

Soon after Devin and Jeremy found a table, the eating began. Roast pork, bread, and cabbage were laid out in front of them. Their days in the open air had brought their hunger alive. Devin was still filling up when a fiddler stood up and played a rollicking jig. A harpist followed and then a storyteller.

The stories of heroic deeds filled Devin with courage. Always the Irish had been brave fighters. Hadn't Devin himself learned the words of Cormac MacArt, a high king of Ireland? "I was fierce in the battlefield," he told his son. "I was gentle in friendship."

Devin felt proud of that fierceness in battle and glad for the Irish around him. Listening to their stories, Devin thought of his last words to his sister. "Courage to win, Bree. Courage to win."

Now Devin wanted everyone to know about Bree's courage. As warmth and good food loosened his tongue, Devin stood up.

Speaking in a voice that all could hear, Devin began

his tale of the two sisters. With bold words he told the story of Keely, taken away by Vikings years before. And now, his sister Bree, also stolen by men who raided the monastery at Glendalough.

Around him, Devin saw the men clench their fists, heard their rumble of anger. Glad for their strong Irish sympathy, Devin kept on. With the telling of the story his own anger grew, as well as his hatred for the Vikings.

When he finished and sat down, a man jumped up and raised a toast. "To Devin, the boy with the soul of a poet, the tongue of a storyteller. To Devin, the storyteller with two sisters lost."

Their faces filled with anger, other men leaped to their feet. "Where are they, lad? Where are these cruel raiders who invaded our land?"

When Devin stood again, every person in the great hall fell silent. In the hush that surrounded him, Devin spoke with a pain that fell like water upon green fields.

"You are brave men bent on rescue," he said. "You are men of courage. But the Viking ship is already far out, somewhere on the stormy North Sea."

A groan went through the hall. No matter how angry they were, even the bravest Irishman knew the ship was beyond reach.

When Devin sat down again, he felt shaky inside. While talking, his anger and hatred for the Vikings had grown. He felt years away from the moment he lay on the rocks next to the Irish Sea, looked up at the stars, and believed that God held him in the hollow of His hand. Was that only a few nights ago?

When a young man started singing a ballad, Devin tried to forget his anger. Instead, he felt uneasy and wondered why. As he looked around, he noticed a man sitting with his back against the wall. As Devin glanced in his direction, the man quickly looked away. Devin used that moment to study him.

With his blond hair and blue eyes the man could be Irish. He could also be a Viking. Whoever he was, his skin was weathered by wind and sun.

For some reason the man had been watching him. Deep inside, Devin had felt that gaze upon him. As a young boy hunting in the forest near his home, Devin had learned not to ignore that feeling. But now he felt puzzled. As far as he knew, he had never seen the man before. Until Devin stood up to speak, the man had no way of knowing him.

Or does he know me? In the stranger's face there was an anger that warned Devin. Suddenly he guessed what it was. *For some reason that man hates me, just like I hate Vikings.*

FOUR

When Bree woke up she had no idea where she was. At first she felt surprised that she no longer felt the motion of the Viking ship. Then, as she saw the cluster of oak and hazel trees around her, she felt stranger still. Sunlight shone between the branches. A large boulder and a circle of smaller rocks tucked her and Lil away.

They didn't find us, Bree told herself.

Slowly, hardly daring to believe what had happened, Bree repeated the thought to herself. Filled with wonder, her excitement grew. *They didn't find us!*

Like a song on the wind Bree heard her thoughts and wondered if she had cried them aloud. *They really didn't find us!*

Lying on the ground nearby, Lil slept with only her face showing. Her reindeer hide blanket surrounded the rest of her head.

For a moment Bree watched Lil and wished she herself could be eight years old again. With all her heart Bree wanted someone to take care of her—to have someone look after her instead of being the one to look after Lil.

Beneath her own reindeer hide blanket, Bree stretched out her legs. Coming more fully awake, she raised her arms high above her head and stretched again. She longed to lie there all day, to doze off and catch up on the sleep she'd lost. Instead, her hunger reminded Bree of all she needed to do.

For as long as she could remember, she had wanted to see the world outside the Wicklow Mountains. That was her quest—what she wanted in life. But then, since being captured by Vikings, Bree wanted only to escape—to go back to the country and family she loved.

Now she knew. *The hardest part of our escape lies ahead.*

It frightened Bree. Until this last week she had always been able to ask her parents for help. Not anymore. Instead, Bree's thoughts flew in every direction. What was she thinking of—to believe she could do this? To not only take care of herself but also someone five years younger?

Then Bree remembered her father's words. "I can't always be with you, but God can."

Right now, there was nothing Bree wanted more than to have her parents with her. As she thought about her family, she remembered her mam saying, "When you feel alone, talk with God."

Though Lil slept nearby, Bree felt very alone, and God seemed far away. In fact, He didn't even seem real. Instead, all the things Bree needed to do pressed down upon her.

Pulling her blanket up around her shoulders, Bree started to pray. "Please, God, I need to know that You are real. Will You help me figure out what to do?"

When she finished praying, Bree tried to put her thoughts in order.

Water. In the dark of night, God had shown them a stream of water.

Shelter. Bree looked around. God had provided that too. He had tucked them away in the hollow of the rocks.

Food. In order to make their escape last, they must eat and keep up their strength. That meant that at least one of them—and she was the oldest—had to leave their hiding place to find food. Whenever she did, she'd run the risk of discovery. Anyone could follow her back.

With all her heart Bree wanted to get as far from Mikkel as possible. But Bree had no idea where to go. And where could they get food?

Fish. Cod. The water was filled with it. There had to be some way to get food and not be recognized. But how?

As Bree lay there thinking, her stomach growled again. And then she knew.

They'll have to see us without seeing us.

Bree grinned. Long ago, she and her younger sister Keely had often made a game of thinking up disguises. Sometimes their brother Devin joined them, but always it was Bree who went back to the game, either in her thoughts or in trying out a disguise.

Now Bree remembered a disguise she had always wanted to use. But she had never guessed how serious the game might become.

During the long days of sailing to Norway, Bree had studied the Vikings and thought about how they looked. Blue eyes, blond or light brown hair. Sometimes red hair. Or reddish blond like her own.

Some had short hair, cut like Mikkel's to just below his ears. Others had long hair, almost as long as Bree's. And like hers, it was sometimes wavy. But so far Bree hadn't seen a Viking with her reddish blond hair and deep brown eyes. Maybe somewhere there was such a person. But if not, it would give her trouble.

So how could she hide the color of her eyes? That was something she could do nothing about. Or was it?

When a man in the Wicklow Mountains injured one of his eyes, he had no choice but to wear an eye patch. When he told Bree about it, he was still filled with bitterness. "When I meet people, all they see is the eye patch. It's like they're drawn to it. They don't see the rest of me."

They don't see the rest of me. If she wore a patch, everyone would look at that instead of her other deep brown eye. What else could she do?

Bree thought about the rest of her disguise. It had to be something she wasn't. Something that made her look so different that no one would think of a thirteen-year-old girl. How could she look older than she was?

Most of the older people Bree knew were able to do countless things that she couldn't manage. She had to pick a disguise that fit her need to fish. If she looked like someone who liked to fish, maybe people wouldn't pay attention to her. And that was just what she wanted!

With that thought she knew exactly what to do. She only had to find a way to do it. And what about Lil?

Short and slender, Lil was small boned and fragile looking. Her skin was clear and white, and she had blue eyes. But her lashes and hair were the black of the dark Irish. The black hair with the blue eyes could give them trouble. And there was something more. Lil looked as if the wind could blow her away. Someone would notice Lil just because she was so small.

Could she pass for a boy? Bree didn't think so. But then again—

Hmmm. This would be harder than thinking up a

disguise for herself. And most difficult of all, they had little or nothing to use.

But then Bree remembered. As though they were in the same room, Bree heard her mother speak. "Let nothing be wasted." In all their lives the O'Toole family had never wasted one egg, one loaf of bread, one square of peat for the fire.

To Bree's mam the rest followed. If you didn't waste, the Lord would provide.

Sometimes neighbors told Mam, "Ach! Maureen O'Toole! Every beggar in Ireland knows the path to your door. Sure, and if your family won't go hungry with all the food you give away." But Mam kept on feeding the hungry. Often she told Bree, "It's the Lord Himself that we serve. He'll take care of us. The Lord will provide."

As clearly as a bell ringing in her ears, Bree heard the words. *The Lord will provide.* Like a promise it came to her. She could ask Him for help. She would need it. Both she and Lil needed food.

Pushing aside her blanket, Bree reached for her shoes and pulled them on. From a space between the rocks, she pulled out the piece of sealskin she had carried with her. Carefully she unrolled it, took out the flatbread she had hidden away, and counted five pieces.

Setting aside two pieces, Bree rolled up the skin. As she tucked it back in its place, Lil opened her eyes and sat up. Even in the dim light, her eyes were the bluest Bree had ever seen. And her lashes? So black that they could make life very hard for both of them.

"Time to eat," Bree said briskly and held out a piece of flatbread.

Lil grinned. "We'll have a feast. I've got two pieces of cheese." Digging deep, she pulled them out and gave one piece to Bree.

Telling herself she had to savor each bite, Bree held the cheese to her mouth. Then she remembered. At home her father always prayed before meals. Now the warm memory of that time around the table made Bree lonesome. Swallowing hard, she closed her eyes before her tears could spill over.

But it was Lil who prayed. "Thank You, Father, for helping us escape. Thank You for this warm house—"

Bree opened her eyes. *Warm house?* For Lil their hideaway had taken on some miraculous qualities. But then Bree saw Lil looking with wonder at the rocks and sheltering oaks. Quickly Bree bowed her head again.

"And thank You, Father," Lil went on, "for this food we eat and all the food You will give us. Amen."

Looking up, Bree met Lil's eyes. During their flight up the mountain Bree had needed to slow down for the younger girl. Bree had even wondered if she did the right thing by taking her. But now there was something Bree knew. When it came to believing God, Lil had just jumped out ahead of her.

Leaning forward, Bree looked into the younger girl's eyes. "You know something? We've been so busy surviving that I don't know the name of your family."

"I'm a Byrne," Lil answered.

"Really?" Bree asked. "You're related to Tully?"

Just speaking his name, Bree felt the deep-down pain of the past week. Like the water pouring over the stepping-stones in the river near her home, a flood of memories came back. With them came Bree's anger about all that had happened.

As if she was there, Bree remembered her birthday morning. As she came down the mountain, Bree had thought she saw the son of her daddy's good friend. Tully . . . standing on a rock with his back toward her, then walking out on the stepping-stones across a dangerous river.

Tully, Bree thought, filled with the pain she had felt so often since. But it had really been Mikkel. Mikkel who betrayed the entire Irish countryside by bringing in his band of Vikings to raid and steal.

Trying not to think about Mikkel, Bree pushed her thoughts away. "You're related to Tully?" she asked again.

Lil grinned. "He's my cousin. That's why I know who you are. He told me about you."

"He did?"

"He wants to marry you someday."

Bree choked. "Tully said that?"

"Tully said that." As though the whole responsibility for their escape rested on her, Lil sat up straight. "So I better get you back to Ireland. Tully will thank me all his livelong days."

"And I will too!" Bree laughed, filled with hope at the thought of stepping foot on the green sod of Ireland. "I'll thank you with all my heart!"

When they finished eating, Bree reached between the rocks and pulled out another bundle. Moments before Bree and Lil left the ship, an Irish woman named Nola had pushed the bundle toward Bree.

"You're going to run, aren't you?" Nola whispered. "Take this when you go."

On board ship Nola had become Bree's friend. With her ability to sew clothing from sealskin, Nola had become everyone's friend.

Now Bree knew that the sealskin she unwrapped was left over when Nola made sure that every girl got a warm garment. The tunic—a simply made dress that hung loosely to the ankles—fit over the dress each girl already wore. The minute Bree put hers on, she had felt warmer.

Bree also felt sure that Nola had given her the last available bit of sealskin. Laying it down on top of her reindeer hide blanket, Bree undid the knot and opened the bundle.

Inside the first sealskin were two more. Then came a small bone case with a large needle and the kind of heavy thread they had used to make clothing on board ship. Next seven pieces of flatbread and five pieces of cheese. Hadn't Nola eaten anything at all?

Then a shawl—a wool shawl of dark blue. If opened completely it was like a square knitted blanket. Folded with one pointed corner to another, the shawl became a triangle worn over a woman's shoulders. Immediately Bree thought of a hundred ways she could use it. She'd have to make sure she knew the best.

And strangely enough, a knitted cap of the kind that many Vikings wore. Green with a white design, it fit like a stocking that went up to a point at the top of the head.

Snatching it up, Bree set the cap on Lil's head. Best of all, the cap was too big for the girl. "Push your hair up inside," Bree told her.

The cap still fit without looking stretched out of shape. Leaning forward, Bree pulled the front of the cap low down over Lil's eyebrows.

"It'll work!" she said. "If you stay out of bright sunlight you'll be fine."

Next came a small stone. Bree looked at it and wondered why it was there. It was a common enough stone, the kind her daddy used to start a fire. At one of the stops along the way had Nola picked it up, just in case? Did she want to make sure Bree remembered what was needed?

One carefully wrapped package still lay on the bottom of the bundle. At first Bree thought that Nola had given her all the leftover scraps of sealskin. That she had. Whatever small, strange shape was left from cutting the large pieces, it was there. But there was also more.

Nola had also managed to cut strips. Long strips that could be used for rope or—Bree stopped unwinding, just thinking about it. But Lil hurried her on.

"What else is there?"

Whatever was inside, it was long and narrow. With each bit of sealskin Bree unwound, her hope grew. Was it what she thought? Could it possibly be? Of course not!

But it was. It truly was.

When the last bit fell away, Bree leaned back on her heels, unable to believe what she saw.

FIVE

BREE'S DISGUISE

Staring at Nola's gift, Bree felt amazed. *I can clean fish! I can make a fire!*

Before Bree lay a leather sheath holding a knife. Not too small, not too large. Just the right size to help her in all the ways they needed to survive.

A knife was something Bree had always treated with respect. With a seven-year-old brother and two younger sisters, Bree understood why her mother kept her kitchen knives on a high shelf. During the daily lessons in which Mam taught her to cook, Bree learned to use those knives well.

When Bree walked with her father in the forest, she learned another kind of respect. All her life Bree had seen

Daddy carry such a knife in a sheath on his belt. His knife was also a tool but used in a great number of ways. Aidan O'Toole couldn't do his work without it.

Once Bree had said, "Why don't you teach me to use your knife?"

"You're a girl, Bree," her brother Dev had teased. "Why do you need to use a man's knife?" Yet even when Bree was younger she believed it was important that she know, though she didn't have a reason why.

Bree's father didn't forget her request. Once he showed Bree how to clean a fish. Another time, when they were deep in the forest, he showed her how to find dry tinder and the best wood for starting a fire. On still another walk into the Wicklow Mountains, he taught her how to cut a green branch for cooking fish over a fire. Year after year her daddy had taken out his knife to fix things. Always Bree watched.

Now as Bree stared at a knife much like his, she felt stunned. How was Nola able to give her a knife? It was beyond Bree's imagination to even guess how her friend had managed.

When she and Nola sewed garments for the girls on the boat, they had borrowed Mikkel's knife. Standing next to Nola, Mikkel had watched until she gave it back to him.

"Do you think this knife is Mikkel's?" Bree asked Lil.

But then she knew that it couldn't be. Mikkel's knife

seemed larger, and he always wore it in the sheath on his belt. Besides, Mikkel had used his knife after loaning it to Nola. Thinking back, Bree had a clear picture of Mikkel high in the rigging on the day of a storm. As the wind howled around them, he clung to the mast. Taking his knife he slashed at the rope that held the sail in place.

Bree swallowed hard, just thinking about that moment. Before the rope gave way, a powerful gust of wind caught the sail, tipping the boat far over on its side. For one terrible moment Mikkel clung for his life as he hung out over the water. Much as Bree hated Mikkel, she didn't want to see him die.

No, this wasn't Mikkel's knife. Whoever it belonged to, Nola had known how much she'd need a knife. Just thinking about the goodness of her kind Irish friend, Bree felt grateful.

Bree set to work at once. Using the knife and a flat rock, she cut the pieces of sealskin she needed. Then, taking a big needle and strong thread, she started sewing. When Bree was finished, she had a hat with a floppy brim that covered her forehead and most of her hair.

Next Bree shaped a small scrap of sealskin into a circle and poked two holes along the edge. After unraveling a side of the shawl she pushed a piece of yarn through each hole and tied it.

Lil was curious. "What are you doing?"

Bree grinned. "I'll surprise you." She was having fun. If this weren't so serious—

By now Bree's sealskin tunic had dried enough to work with it. The loose-fitting tunic fit over her dress and almost reached her ankles. With Lil's help Bree cut the tunic to end just above her knees. With the extra sealskin and pieces from Nola's bundle, Bree made leggings for Lil.

Quickly Bree sewed the seams, and Lil pulled on her new clothing. The leggings fit loosely, and Bree tied short strips of leather around Lil's ankles. Lil used another of Nola's strips of leather to make a drawstring for her waist. With two squares of sealskin and more leather strips Bree made boots that came up over Lil's ankles.

When Bree finished sewing her own leggings, she took part of her reindeer hide blanket to make a short cloak. In the middle of the square piece Bree cut a hole large enough for her head to slip through.

Quickly Bree put on her new clothes, then said, "Let's look around!"

By now the midday sun was high overhead. As it sifted through the oak leaves, Bree saw the light and tried to tell herself that nothing really bad could happen. Inside their hiding place she felt safe—at least for the moment. But now, as she and Lil stepped outside their tucked-away hollow, Bree stopped, waited, and looked in every direction.

"If there's anyone around, we have to separate," she warned Lil. "Mikkel and his men are used to seeing us together."

They had come to this spot when it was dark, and Bree needed a moment to be sure her directions were right. When she felt she knew the way, they climbed up the slope first and stayed on rocky ground to hide their footprints. Then, when they were far enough away from their shelter, they found firm ground and grass.

As they walked toward the stream, Bree kept looking around. Before long, she heard the sound of falling water and knew she had found the place. Bree and Lil washed their faces and hands, then drank deeply of the clear, cold water.

On the way back to their hiding place, they walked toward the light between the trees. When they stood on the side of the mountain, Bree felt stunned by the view below them. Only then did she realize how high they had climbed the night before.

Far, far, below, a wide stream led from the sea into a round body of water that looked like a large lake. Near the shore were a number of buildings of a size that made Bree wonder if it was a king's farm. Large fields of grain surrounded the buildings.

In the opposite direction and to Bree's right was the harbor where Mikkel's ship had come in the day before. From here Bree could see that the ships were drawn up on a peninsula. Near the cluster of houses she and Lil had passed was the line of trees where they hid.

"Look!" Lil pointed. "That's where the dogs nearly found us."

Bree shivered, just thinking about it. Around the houses there seemed to be small farms with fields and grazing land.

Now Bree tried to put her fear aside. The day before, she had learned that the harbor was surrounded by seven mountains. The beauty of all she saw filled her with awe. Was there another place like it in the entire world?

It makes me lonesome," Lil said. "Lonesome for Ireland."

"Me too," answered Bree. Whenever she could, Bree had climbed to her favorite spot on the mountain behind her home. Always the distant waters of the Irish Sea had drawn Bree in a way she couldn't explain even to herself. *If only I could know what's out there,* she had thought countless times.

For as long as she could remember, Bree had been curious to know about life in faraway places. Now she smiled at her dream. If only she had known how she'd travel!

Here, even from such a great height, Bree could tell which ship was Mikkel's. It lay closest to the sea, and men, women, and children moved about like tiny, make-believe people.

Men carried long pieces of wood from the ship. In just a few minutes they put uprights and crosspieces in place, then spread cloth over the framework to make a tent. Other men carried more wood from the ship. As they fit pieces of wood together, Bree strained forward to see. Were they really setting up traveling beds?

At first Bree felt fascinated. Then she understood what was happening. Since the Vikings hadn't found her and Lil, they weren't leaving for home. They were making themselves comfortable.

The truth of it pounded away at Bree's heart. *They won't sail on till they find us. If needed, they'll keep looking forever.*

"It's scary, isn't it?" Lil whispered, and Bree knew. Though Lil was five years younger, she understood exactly what they were seeing.

For over a week Bree had asked herself how to outwit Mikkel and his men. Even so, there had been times when being captured by Vikings didn't seem quite real. But now Bree felt sure of one thing. Mikkel and his men would never allow her to win. They would do everything in their power to bring her and Lil back. And if they did—

Bree didn't want to think about it.

"I will protect you," Mikkel had promised when Bree told him he owed her something. "But you must obey me."

By escaping, Bree had not obeyed him. Just thinking

about what could happen if she and Lil were found, Bree trembled.

"We need two things," she told Lil. "A place to go and enough food to get there."

If they were to eat, Bree had no choice but to return to the harbor. Again she remembered. *They must see us without seeing us.*

First they must complete their disguises. On a nearby slope there was sunlight and patches of grass between the rocks.

Staying as close to the trees as possible, Bree started breaking off blades of grass. Lil dropped each handful inside her leggings, then drew the drawstring around her waist. When she held out her arms and turned around for inspection, Lil laughed. She seemed to have gained at least fifteen pounds.

In the short time since they'd escaped from the Viking ship, Lil had become a different person. In spite of their danger, Lil had become the lighthearted girl she had probably been at home.

While Lil stayed in the hollow of the rocks, Bree went out again, this time to collect what she needed. Soon she saw a long branch on the ground. Though a windfall, the wood looked strong. Bree broke off the side branches and soon had the strong walking stick she needed.

Next Bree found a supple branch long enough for a

fishing pole. Again she trimmed it to size. Then she turned around and started back to their hiding place.

As always, Bree chose a route that was different from the last way she walked. Long ago her daddy had taught Bree to not make a beaten-down path to their home. And that was how she stumbled across the remains of a cooking fire.

Bree stopped and looked around. The fire ring was surrounded by stones set in a large patch of dirt. Whoever cooked there had made a round pit dug like a shallow basin into the earth. Only a few pieces of charred wood remained.

Pushing aside her new cloak, Bree opened a small bag at her waist. Taking out a tiny mirror of polished brass, she propped it against a stone and reached for her comb. Seconds later she decided to leave her hair the way it was.

With her fingertips Bree touched the charred wood and drew a line from each ear to just below her nose. Carefully she rubbed black down the lower sides of her face. If she stayed out of the sunlight, maybe the shadow would look as if she needed to shave.

Next Bree drew her hands across her cloak, leggings, and shoes. Then she ran dirty fingers through her hair and hid the ends under her cloak.

Finally Bree looked again into her mirror. When she smiled, her lips seemed out of place in the new face she had created. Her hair looked straggly and her clothes were filthy. Could she manage to fool the Vikings who searched for her?

On the way back to Lil, Bree washed her hands at the stream, then remembered the final piece of her disguise. From a tucked-away pocket she took the small round piece of sealskin she had cut. With the patch over her right eye, Bree tied the yarn around the back of her head and set her hat in place. If she kept the hat drawn low, maybe no one would notice her other dark brown eye.

When Bree entered their hiding place, Lil looked up, caught sight of Bree, and gasped. Fear leaped into her eyes.

Bree spoke quickly. "It's just me."

Lil tried to cover her fright. "When you talk, I know that, but you're so real!"

Reaching out, Bree hugged her, but the small, slender girl still trembled.

"To you I will always talk," Bree said gently. "But with everyone else I must remember that I cannot."

Bree felt terrible that she had frightened the younger girl. But Lil took a deep whiff of the charred wood. "Whew!" she exclaimed, backing away. "You stink! My cousin won't want to marry you now!"

That afternoon Bree sewed a bag for carrying fish, then unraveled more of the shawl Nola had given them. With the yarn Bree made a fishing line and attached it to the branch she had cut in the woods. Then Bree shaped the rest of the shawl into a boy's sweater for Lil.

As the shadows grew long and it became difficult to see, Bree realized that she still needed a fishing hook. She could find a small branch with a crook and use the knife to shape it. But she was running out of time and light.

Then, from a peaceful day of walking along the Irish Sea, Bree remembered. In places where fishing was good, someone always dropped a hook. If she looked along the shore and found a hook or two, it would help her recognize a good spot to fish.

Hours later, Bree woke in the darkness of night and knew it was time to leave. Yet even the idea of returning to the harbor was more than she could handle.

"Lil, I'm scared," Bree whispered. "Really scared. How did I ever think I could fool the Vikings?"

"You thought it because you needed to," Lil whispered back.

Listening to Lil's calm voice, Bree felt better. Lil was right. They needed two things before they could leave this place—food and somewhere to go.

But Lil started praying. "Jesus, we ask You to protect Bree. And help her find out what we need to know."

After a quick hug, Bree slipped out of the shelter. Feeling grateful for the full moon, she started down the mountain.

At first Bree walked quickly. Soon she discovered that with one eye covered, trees seemed to be in a slightly different place. When she didn't feel sure of her footing, Bree pushed up her eye patch.

Before long, the front of her legs ached from going downhill too fast. Whenever possible, she stayed near the edge of the trees where there was more light. Even so, the darkness crept back into Bree's heart. The dangers of what she planned to do seemed overwhelming.

She must stay as far as possible from the Viking ships. She must leave before dawn. And she must refuse to talk. Every moment would be filled with danger.

Again Bree thought back to the games she used to play with her sister Keely. The one they liked best was when they pretended to be someone else. Usually Keely wanted to be a chieftain's wife. Bree always tried something harder—a part totally unlike who she really was. Now Bree reminded herself what she must do if she was going to look like an old fisherman.

Could she remember to walk with slow steps instead of her own quick movements? She could never forget the part she was playing. That might be the moment when Mikkel or another Viking watched.

When she reached the bottom of the mountain, Bree looked around, then pulled the patch down over her right eye. Directly ahead lay one end of the harbor. The cluster of houses lay at the opposite end and some distance away. Everything was still dark, just as Bree hoped.

As the smell of the sea mingled with the dampness of

night, Bree crossed the open area between trees and water. With each step her worry grew. Then she remembered her brother Dev. "Courage to win, Bree," he had often told her.

Now Bree needed that courage, not just for herself, but also for Lil. Yet there was one thing that Bree knew. She didn't have courage by herself. She needed the Lord's help.

It was low tide, and Bree searched above the waterline for mussels that clung to the rocks. In the moonlight she gathered as many as she needed and stowed them away for bait. Then Bree walked along the shore, searching for fishing hooks someone might have dropped.

Again the light of the moon helped her out. When Bree caught sight of not one, but two hooks, she had all she could do to not pounce on them. Bending down like an old man, she picked up the hooks, then looked for a spot to fish.

A large boulder near the edge of the water offered Bree good protection from people at the other end of the harbor. Sitting down in the shadow of the boulder, Bree rigged her line, baited the hook, and flicked it into the water.

As the darkness held, Bree caught several fish. One after another, she slipped the cod into the bag on the ground next to her. Before long, she felt ready to make her escape back up the mountain.

But then Bree heard the crunch of someone walking

across the small stones along the beach. Moments later, the person sat down on a nearby rock.

Bree's muscles tightened. Whoever it was, the person was only a short distance away. If that person made the wrong move—

Bree thought about it. She needed to reach the trees before first light. Could she gather her pole and fish, jump up fast, and get away?

Reaching out with her free hand, Bree drew the top of the bag over her most recently caught fish. Turning her head slightly, she tried to see out the corner of her eye. But then whoever was there moved directly behind her.

A moment later the person spoke. "Old man, you're really a girl, aren't you?"

SIX

ONE LIVING THING

Bree grew very still. Without moving even an eyelid, she listened.

"I heard the Vikings talk about you. You want to escape, don't you?"

Still Bree waited, unwilling to give herself away. Whoever this person was, she could just be guessing.

But the woman spoke again. "Your disguise is perfect except for one thing."

Bree's heart pounded.

"Your disguise is very clever. But your hands are too small, too white, too clean."

Instantly Bree put her free hand inside her cloak. But the other hand remained on the pole she held.

"Yes, keep them out of sight when you can."

Turning, Bree caught a glimpse of a woman with flaming red hair. *Hmmm,* Bree thought. *Is she the owner of the barking dogs? Did she purposely let us get away?*

Bree looked back at her fishing pole and stared at the spot where her line disappeared into the water.

"Rub your hands in dirt," the woman said. "Keep them dirty, no matter how much you hate it."

Laying down her pole, Bree reached out and dug into the dirt next to the rock where she sat. Carefully she rubbed the dirt onto one hand, then the other.

But the woman's soft voice went on. And now Bree heard it. The manner of speaking. A turn of the words. The way of the Irish. Though the woman spoke the Norse language, Bree heard the difference.

Turning her head just slightly, Bree spoke softly. "You're Irish."

"I'm Rowena," the woman answered. "I was once a slave, but I grew to love the man who took me captive. I married him."

Laughter filled her voice. "He's a strong, wonderful Norwegian."

Bree couldn't think of anything more awful than marrying the person who had hurt her that much. Though two other lads had captured her, Mikkel had planned the raid that took Bree from her family. She was sure of one thing: She hated Mikkel. She could never possibly respect him. Why would anyone even want him for a friend?

"There's a difference between Norwegians," Rowena said, as though hearing Bree's thoughts. Now Rowena spoke in the Irish. "Do you know that?"

Bree shook her head. All she had ever heard about were the cruel Vikings—warlike men who invaded Ireland and took whatever they wanted. Captives made them wealthy.

"There are Vikings who take the easy way out," Rowena went on. "In their fast boats they dart out from the bays to rob passing ships. Often they're younger sons who will not inherit land."

Again Bree thought of Mikkel. On the trip to Norway he and Hauk, the man who was his teacher, talked about it.

"Other times they're just men who are greedy. But most Norwegians are peace loving. They're farmers and fisherman and sometimes traders."

Wanting to be sure she didn't miss one word, Bree turned her head still more.

"If you go across the mountains, you'll find a hut by the sea. If you get there, they are true merchants—Norwegians who trade their goods honestly and fairly. They will take you back to Ireland."

Quickly Rowena gave directions. Then she was gone.

Anxious to flee, Bree gathered up her things. Before

she could leave, the crunch of stones told Bree she had another visitor. Whoever it was stopped some distance away.

Hunching her shoulders, Bree huddled in the shadow of the boulder. It took all her willpower to stare at her pole as though caring only about the fish that she caught.

As she waited, afraid to move, a mist rose from the water and clung to the top of the mountains. Would the mist and darkness be enough to hide her escape?

Then Bree's pole jerked down. In the still water the circles around her line moved outward. Bree raised her pole, swung the line toward her, and caught the flapping fish. It took only a moment to take the fish off the hook and drop it into the bag. As Bree baited the hook again, her hands trembled.

This won't do.

Still Bree felt that someone was there. Still she knew that she could not turn and look. Her fear growing by leaps and bounds, Bree counted to ten. Next she named all the people in her family and clung to their faces. By then she'd caught another fish.

Once more Bree lifted the line and took the fish from the hook as if she did this every day of her life. Again she heard the crunch of feet on small stones. Some distance down the beach, a person spoke.

"See anything?" That was Mikkel.

At first Bree thought he was talking to her, but she

refused to turn. Whoever was with Mikkel must have shrugged, for Bree heard no reply. One person? Two? She wasn't sure.

"No one at all?" Mikkel's voice carried well on the water.

"Just an old man with a mess of fish."

Gunnar, Bree thought. *The guard with the cruel light in his eyes.* More than once Bree had picked out his voice.

"Nothing on the mountain?" Mikkel asked.

"Not even a footprint."

Gunnar again. The night of Bree's escape he had watched her side of the ship. That is, until the heavens opened and a strong wind slashed the rain sideways. Then all four guards slipped under the lowered sail. To Bree's relief they had gone aboard at the other end of the boat.

"We'll find them," Mikkel said.

"The younger girl?" Gunnar asked. "I never paid attention to how she looks."

"Black hair, deep blue eyes, small and thin. A wind would blow her away."

Gunnar's laugh was hard and cold. "If we find her—"

"If you find either of them, treat them well." Mikkel's voice held no doubt about it.

Treat us well? Bree's thoughts filled with bitterness. *Tie us up again, you mean. Keep us as slaves for as long as we live.* Bree decided she had never hated Mikkel as much as in that moment. Then she heard another voice.

"I can't believe it's Bree. She wouldn't steal."

Steal? Bree's heart flipped faster than a fish escaping its hook. They wanted her for stealing? Not just for running away?

"That's where you're wrong, Alf," Gunnar answered. "Anyone will steal if the temptation is big enough."

Alf? Bree searched her mind but couldn't remember a Viking named Alf. Who was this man who believed she wouldn't steal? She couldn't place his quiet voice. Then she heard it again.

"Bree is too nice a girl to steal." Alf sounded sure about that. "It's the trolls, I tell you. They live in these mountains."

"Trolls!" mocked Gunnar. "How can you possibly believe in trolls?"

"Don't make them angry! If you get on the wrong side of trolls, you never know what they'll do!"

Gunnar laughed. "Maybe they'll get *you,* but they aren't going to get me. I'm smarter than any old troll!"

Mikkel's hard voice broke in. "You're wasting time. Keep searching. But look for Bree, not the trolls."

A moment later Bree again heard the crunch of stones. With every ounce of will that she owned, she did not turn to look. Then she heard footsteps move closer. As the men passed behind her, Alf called out. "Got a good mess of fish, old man?"

Bree's heart thumped. If she didn't turn, maybe he

would think she couldn't hear. She just wanted to flee the harbor.

Instead, Bree waited. The two men had left. But Mikkel? Bree could only feel glad that her eye patch was on the side where he stood.

Then, as though he didn't have a care in the world, Mikkel started to whistle. Again the sound carried well. Bree's panic grew. Darkness and mist hung around her, but how long would it last?

When Bree's left hand started to tremble, she wedged her elbow against her body. But the pole wobbled, and even her right hand couldn't steady it. Just as Bree felt sure that Mikkel would see, the line jerked down, bringing the end of the pole with it.

Mikkel stopped whistling. Was he leaving? Was he coming her way?

Bree's panic overwhelmed her. She wanted only to stand up and start running. To flee to their hiding place as fast as she could go. Then she remembered her father's words.

"I can't always be with you, but God can."

God can.

As if nothing in the world was as important as bringing in that fish, Bree kept her eyes straight ahead. Lifting her pole, she swung the line toward her. But her thoughts were of Brother Cronan, her teacher in the monastery school at Glendalough.

Cronan translated the Latin of the Bible into the everyday language that Bree, Devin, and other Irish knew. When Cronan asked them to memorize the words of the Bible, they usually learned one verse at a time. But Bree often went beyond that to memorize whole sections of the Bible.

More than once Cronan had told her, "Child, God has given you a very special gift. If you hear a verse once, you understand what it says. If you hear it twice, you remember it."

When he first spoke of it, Bree felt awed by his words. Before long, she knew Cronan was right. But Bree also knew that unusual ability did not belong to her. It was just what Brother Cronan called it—a gift from the heart of God.

Now, Bree felt grateful for that gift. Closing her hand around a good-sized cod, she took it off the hook. And then in the stillness she remembered God's promise in the book of Hebrews. "Never will I leave you; never will I forsake you."

In that moment Bree knew she could say with confidence, "The Lord is my helper; I will not be afraid. What can man do to me?"

As Bree's hands grew steady, she waited. Mist and darkness still hung over the harbor. Mikkel still stood some distance away. And Bree still pretended that she didn't notice.

Then Mikkel walked away.

"Thank You, Lord," Bree whispered.

But deep inside there was something she knew. *Mikkel will not stop searching until he finds me.*

Once again the line jerked down. Bree lifted the pole, swung the line toward her, and reached out for a big cod. But the hook slipped free. The fish wiggled out of her hold and flipped back into the water.

Bree sagged with relief, glad to see at least one living thing go free.

SEVEN

RED SHIRT

In the great hall of the public house, the voices rose and fell around Bree's brother, Devin. Who was this man whose face was filled with hate? Again Devin wondered if he could be a Viking.

The great hall was warm now. Most of the men and boys had taken off their cloaks, but the man along the wall still wore his. Instead of linen or wool, it was made of a soft leather that looked like sealskin. That, too, could be Irish, and a man's cloak often told his wealth or lack of it.

A round brooch, a silver pin at the man's shoulder, held his cloak in place. But then, as the man moved his arms, the cloak opened. Devin saw the red shirt underneath.

A knot formed at the pit of Devin's stomach. Both Vikings and Irish loved bright colors. The man hiding in the bushes by the Irish Sea wore such a shirt. So, too, did the man running on the road. Was this the same man?

In that moment Devin knew he had made a terrible mistake. Never should he have talked about Bree and Keely, the sisters carried away by Vikings. By telling about them, he had given himself away as Bree's brother, the lad set free by Mikkel.

Then Devin remembered. For his entire time on the longship he had been tied up, lying on the deck. He had been down behind a sea chest, so he had seen the faces of only a few Vikings. Reaching over, Devin touched Jeremy's arm.

When the boy turned, Devin spoke softly. "Don't look now, but do you recognize the man along the wall? The one wearing a leather cloak?"

As soon as Jeremy glanced that way, he whispered in Devin's ear. "He looks familiar, but I'm not sure. The Vikings didn't wear cloaks when they worked on the boat. Whoever that man is, he sure looks mean."

Devin thought about it. *How can I know if the man is a Viking?* If he was left behind because I was set free, he'll do everything he can to get even.

Then Devin realized he didn't have to know. Whoever the man was, his face was full of anger and hate. He was Devin's enemy. And the man sat with his back to the wall.

Long ago Devin's father had warned him. "Two kinds of men sit with their backs against the wall. One of them trusts no one. The other wants protection."

Right now Devin wanted protection. Slowly and without sound, he and Jeremy moved toward the wall on the opposite side of the room from the man with the red shirt. When it came time to lie down for the night, both Devin and Jeremy had their backs against the wall. In this place of refuge they had the protection of their host, but neither of the boys wanted to take a chance.

Sometime during the night Devin woke in a cold sweat. His first thought was of Bree. *She's in trouble again.* When he started praying, he knew he should keep on.

The fire had died down, but red still glowed from the logs. As Devin prayed, he wished he could shout to his sister across the ocean that separated them.

Courage to win, Bree, he would tell her. Over the years those words had been their way to help one another. But now Devin felt there was something blocking his prayers. He, the great storyteller, had told the biggest, most awful story of his life. No one could blame him for speaking about his sisters. But he had told their story with hate in his heart.

Already great harm had come of it. Devin had no doubt that his own hate had dropped deep into the heart of the man with the red shirt.

Who is he? Devin wondered again. *If he was left behind, he knows that Mikkel suddenly set sail because of me.*

And Devin knew something else—that hate builds upon hate. More than once his dad had talked about it. And more than once his mam had told Devin to forgive the person who hurt him.

Forgive the Vikings? Forgive the terrible things they had done? Devin wouldn't even think about it.

Instead, he remembered Bree. What was happening to her? Devin had no way of knowing. He could only see into his own heart, and it was filled with hate. And Devin seemed unable to pray.

Nearby, a man lay snoring. Farther off, someone tossed in his sleep. But Devin was afraid. Afraid for himself and Jeremy. Even more, afraid for Bree.

At the center of the large room the logs turned to embers and broke apart. But Devin still lay awake, unable to sleep.

After he finally dozed off, Devin woke up feeling a warning deep inside. On his way to the public house, he had sensed that kind of warning. Now, lying in the dark, Devin looked up at a ceiling he could not see and tried to figure out his feelings.

What woke me? he wondered. Devin wasn't sure, but one thing he knew. As long as he and Jeremy stayed in this house, the man who owned it would protect them. But if they stayed, they would not be able to walk home.

Already Devin's parents had waited long days and nights without knowing what had happened to him. Jeremy's parents, who lived in another part of the Wicklow Mountains, had waited just as long. Their families needed to know that he and Jeremy were safe.

Raising up on one elbow, Devin looked across the hall. The angry looking man in the red shirt lay with his face toward Devin. The sealskin cloak covered him like a blanket. His eyes were closed, and he seemed to be sleeping.

In that moment Devin made up his mind. If they went now, he and Jeremy would be well on their way. If Red Shirt was a left-behind Viking, they could get ahead of him.

Reaching over to where Jeremy lay, Devin tugged his sleeve. "Wake up!" Devin whispered. "We need to leave."

Feeling around in the darkness, Devin found his shoes. As he pulled them on, he again felt the damaged place on his right shoe. Even in the dark, Dev could tell it was growing weaker. But maybe the shoe would last until he got home.

Without making a sound, Devin and Jeremy pulled their small bundles together. As they stood up, a log broke and fell deeper into the hearth. Across the hall, the stranger lifted his head.

Devin froze. Jeremy stood without moving.

Then the stranger lowered his head. When he seemed to be sleeping again, Devin and Jeremy slipped from the hall.

Outside it was still dark, but both boys knew the direction they should take.

By the time dawn came, they were far from the hall and the kind host who had warmed, fed, and sheltered them.

That day it rained often with the mists of Ireland coming and going. With each shower the road grew more soft. Soon the path was well marked by the feet of those who passed from one place to the next.

By late afternoon Devin felt good about the distance they had traveled. They had even managed to escape the stranger with the angry face. In case he followed, they had taken different roads and changed paths often. Even so, they made good time toward home.

When he and Jeremy stopped to rest, Devin looked down at his shoes. For most of the day his right foot had been wet. The strange jagged tear had grown larger.

No matter, Devin thought, sure that his footprints would blend with those of others. But then he looked back at the soft road behind them. First he saw Jeremy's footprints. Then he saw his own. As surely as if he had put up a sign for all to read, his damaged shoe marked a trail.

Devin sighed. So much for being careful. And once again, they needed a place to sleep.

That night Devin and Jeremy crawled under a haystack. As Devin lay there, trying to sleep, one question filled his mind. *How can I help Bree?*

Before long, he thought of a plan. The Viking city of Dublin was on their way home. There Devin could search out a merchant from Norway and ask how to rescue Bree. But with the plan his worry grew. *Who can I trust?*

For two centuries Vikings had come to the shores of Ireland. Their reign of terror centered on monasteries because of the gifts brought by pilgrims. The surrounding countryside also felt the Viking cruelty. Yet between raids, life in Ireland went on pretty much as usual.

Some Vikings married Irish women. Daring sailors from the North had developed a *longphort,* or fortified landing place, at Dublin. In the first true town in Ireland, Christians built churches.

It wasn't the average trader that troubled Devin. Now, near the end of the tenth century, his own father traveled to Dublin to meet with traders from other parts of the world. Instead, Devin dreaded raiders like Mikkel—pirates who stole whatever they could.

"How can we protect ourselves against Red Shirt or any other raider?" Devin asked Jeremy the next morning. Red Shirt had become their name for the angry-looking man.

"If Red Shirt finds us, what will he do?"

"I don't know," Devin had to answer. "I think he wants to get even because Mikkel left him behind. Maybe he'd beat us up. Maybe he'd say we're his slaves. Maybe he would follow us home."

When they talked about it, Devin and Jeremy agreed on what to do. If they were going to help Bree, they must find a safe way in and out of Dublin.

The fog still clung to the hills and sank into the valleys when Devin and Jeremy started walking again. This time Devin took off his shoes.

His feet were tough from years of going barefoot. Yet the rocky path soon left cuts and bruises on his feet.

In the time that followed, Devin and Jeremy walked where the mountains of Mourne swept down to the sea. At night they stayed with whatever family welcomed them. As the boys dropped south to Dublin, they watched and hoped they had left Red Shirt behind.

More than once, flocks of sheep filled the path. Twice a farmer gave them a ride on his cart. Then one afternoon Devin and Jeremy came to a wooded area.

A narrow stream tumbled down the hillside, drawing them there to quench their thirst. From farther away Devin heard water falling from one level to the next.

Near the road was a spring. Devin drank long and deep, hoping the water would fill up his empty stomach.

Then, as he lifted his head from the water, he heard a noise—a faint rustle from not far away. Trying not to appear afraid, Devin stared in that direction.

The green shrubs were thick with enough leaves to

hide anyone who might stand behind them. Moving quickly, Devin slipped into the open and stayed there.

While walking far above the Irish Sea, he felt uneasy again. Prickles went up and down his spine. If he took a wrong step he would land on rocks far below. Anyone could push him off the narrow path.

Trying to make it seem he was just looking around, Devin turned his head. No man lurked behind him. No one ducked down behind a nearby rock. But Devin still felt uneasy. There was no doubt in his mind. Something was wrong.

When Devin reached a wider spot in the path, he suddenly whirled around. This time he caught a shadow that quickly disappeared.

In that moment Devin stopped in the middle of the path and asked, "Jeremy, do you hate the Vikings?"

Jeremy stopped too. "We're not supposed to hate."

"But do you?"

Jeremy nodded. "Bree helped both of us get away. But she's still a prisoner—a slave. How can I *not* hate Mikkel for doing that?"

"That's the way I feel too," Devin said. "So we're agreed. We don't have to forgive."

But Jeremy looked at him with solemn eyes. "Uh-huh."

"What do you mean, 'Uh-huh'?"

"Just that. I think we do have to forgive. But I don't know how. If we forgive those stupid Vikings, are we saying that what they did was all right?"

EIGHT

THE WARNING

In the darkness before dawn Bree watched the fish swim away. Anxious to make her escape, she would have stood up as quickly as her nimble legs allowed. Then she remembered. Pushing her walking stick into the ground, she used it to pull herself up. With her pole and bag of fish over her shoulder, she set off.

Bree had grown used to the rhythm now. Stick down, lean forward, walk ahead. Stick down, lean forward, walk ahead. Stumble a bit. Shuffle forward. Head for the nearest cover.

When she slipped into the edge of the woods, Bree turned to look back. As far as she could tell, no one was looking. But how would she know if someone peered down from above? Or if someone watched from between the branches as she did?

Setting aside her desire to run, Bree walked slowly until well hidden by trees. She was concerned about Lil now. Was she still safe in their tucked-away place?

If something happened to Lil, Bree knew she would never forgive herself. How could she continue to keep her friend safe?

Deep in the woods, Bree picked up her pace, but with every movement she watched and listened. More than once she turned quickly to see if anyone followed.

When Bree reached their hideaway, Lil was excited. "Look what I found!" she said.

Lil held out a soapstone pot. Carved from soft stone, it was a round cooking pot with a handle off to one side.

Bree was excited too. It was just what they needed to boil water. They could have something warm to drink. "Where did you find it?" she asked.

"Near a place where someone built a fire. Not far from where we get water."

Bree had wanted Lil to stay in their hideaway. She was safer there. But now Bree didn't want to spoil her excitement.

The pot was cracked, and iron fasteners held the soapstone together in two places. Perhaps that was the reason why someone left it behind. Even so, if Bree and Lil were careful, it might last a long time.

But then Bree started wondering. Was the pot really left behind? Or had someone put it there as bait to draw them out of hiding?

Bree felt uncomfortable just thinking about it. Still, with a cooking vessel they could boil fish. Maybe someone really did leave the pot behind. Yet Bree didn't want to take a chance. For as long as they hid close by, she, too, would leave the pot at the fire ring.

When Bree went back to the place where someone had built a fire, Lil went with her. "If anyone comes, you must hide at once," Bree warned her again. "They'll recognize us if we're together."

Being together felt good as they searched for dry kindling. After the pounding rain of the night before, Bree wondered if they could find what they needed. Yet a tucked-away spot gave them some long dead grass. In other places they found twigs and pieces of fallen birch bark. They even managed to find windfalls—branches blown down by the wind—that had been sheltered from the rain.

Bree put everything in the fire ring. Peeling apart the layers of birch bark, she set aside the thin papery layer to use as tinder. Then she took out the small rock Nola had given her. With quick striking movements she ran the back of her knife across the rock.

When a spark fell onto the thin pieces of birch bark, Bree leaned close and blew to keep the red glow alive.

Once the bark was burning well, she held grass and small twigs close. She kept adding twigs and thicker birch bark until the fire was hot enough to burn large pieces of wood.

While Lil fed the fire, Bree went to the stream. A short distance from where the water dropped over a ledge, she found a flat rock and began cleaning the fish.

From her earliest childhood Bree had watched her father. Now the memory came back so clearly that it made Bree lonesome for home. After cutting off the head, she slit the fish down one side and pushed out the innards. At first her movements were awkward, and Bree tore the flesh. With each fish her fingers moved more nimbly. By the time she finished washing the pieces, she felt as if she had cleaned fish all her life.

Bree set some of the fish aside. The rest she cut into four or five pieces, then dropped the cod into boiling water. Then she covered the pot with a piece of wood. When the fish was ready, Bree peeled off the skin, and the bones came with it.

As she and Lil sat around the fire, they let the logs burn down to embers. Lil licked her fingers, patted the grass inside her leggings, and grinned. "Look at all the weight I've gained."

Bree teased her. "You like this more than you know."

"It's like a game, isn't it?" Lil asked.

Bree felt surprised, then glad that Lil could feel that way. "Yes, it's like a game."

"A serious game."

Again Bree nodded. She didn't want Lil to know how serious. Nor how dangerous.

"Who's going to win, Bree?"

In that moment Bree felt certain that Lil understood every danger they faced. "Who's going to win?" Bree asked. "I don't know, Lil. I want to believe that we will. But I really don't know."

Then Bree remembered. Long ago she and her brother Devin had worked out a secret sign. A mean boy—a lad older than Dev—lived on the next farm. More than once, the boy had been cruel to both Devin and Bree. On the day he turned eight, Devin knew he had to stand up to him.

"We need a secret sign," Devin told Bree. "A sign that helps me win."

Seven-year-old Bree thought about it. "Mam says that Jesus wants to help us whenever we're scared."

"And Dad says we need to have courage," Devin answered.

"What's courage?" Bree asked.

"Doing the right thing, even if I'm scared."

Just thinking about that day, Bree felt lonesome for her brother. But then she told Lil about the secret sign.

"By yourself you're just an ordinary girl," Bree said. "And I'm just your ordinary friend. But if we ask God to help us—"

Bree crossed her arms over her chest. "When you see this, you'll know that I'm praying for you."

Lil grinned. She, too, crossed her arms over her chest. "And when you see this, you'll know I'm praying for *you.*"

Lil raised her hand and pointed to the sky. "Jesus is our Savior, our Lord, and King."

Bree blinked. "You saw Devin when he left the ship! You heard me talk to Mikkel."

Lil nodded. "I saw. I heard. And whatever happens to me, I believe in Jesus too."

Whatever happens to you? Bree felt the dread of Lil's words. If anything happened to Lil, she would feel the pain deep in her heart. And she would believe it was her fault.

But now Bree had a more immediate problem. How long could they keep fish before it spoiled? Bree wasn't sure. At home her brothers always gobbled everything in sight. Bree only knew that later in the day she and Lil would be hungry again.

Using long green poles, Bree tied them together on one end and rigged a three-legged frame she could set above the embers. After stringing Nola's strips of sealskin around the frame, she cut the remaining fish in long thin pieces and hung them over the glowing coals. Then she wrapped her cloak outside the frame and watched to see if the fish would dry.

Suddenly the fire flared up. Bree barely snatched her

cloak away before it scorched. As the frame tipped, every piece of fish dropped into the fire. Before Bree could get the pieces out, they all burned up.

Bree groaned. Even their evening meal was gone. Lil took one look at her and said, "It's all right. You tried."

But Bree was already thinking about the next morning. There was nothing she wanted to do less than return to the harbor. Even the thought of it set her stomach churning. Yet what else could she do? She and Lil needed another mess of fish. If she cooked it on a stick—cooked it really long and hard—would it last for at least a day or two?

Bree had no idea. She also had no idea if they could find food on their way to the fisherman's hut.

But Lil crossed her arms over her chest, pointed to the sky, and tried to smile. "Courage to win, Bree," she said. "Courage to win."

That night Bree left even earlier than on her first trip to the harbor. Again she collected mussels from the rocks and sat down to fish. She would not run the risk of being there when dawn lit the sky.

Then, as Bree pulled up one fish after another, she heard a voice from behind.

"Old man—"

The Irish woman named Rowena had walked so quietly that Bree had not heard her. Bree turned for a quick glance. Today Rowena wore a hood over her flaming hair.

"Old man, Mikkel visited my husband last night. The tall, thin man named Gunnar was with him."

Without turning, Bree waited, her dread growing.

"Gunnar says that a girl named Bree stole a bag of silver coins. Did you?"

Bree shook her head.

"I didn't think so. Do you know what the law of this land says about a thief?"

Again Bree shook her head.

"In this country the freemen meet at a council called a *ting.* The freemen agree on laws and hold a trial if a person has done something wrong. Whoever commits a crime must pay compensation—something that makes up for the way a thief dishonored the other person. Do you understand?"

"I think so."

"It's believed that when a person steals, he is too poor to pay compensation. Even if the thief gives back what he stole, he is not able to pay extra money to the person he hurt."

Bree's stomach was churning now. "Go on."

"If a thief can't pay compensation for dishonoring someone else, the punishment for theft is death."

When Bree's trembling began, she could not stop it. She could only lay her fishing pole on the ground. "And they think I stole the bag of silver coins."

"I cannot ask you to my house. My husband will guess who you are. But I brought you bread and cheese."

Rowena moved close, passed a bundle to Bree, then moved away from her again.

Bree thrust the bundle under her cloak and tied it with the leather strip holding up her leggings. Two loaves of bread. A large slab of cheese. It seemed a miracle.

Rowena repeated her directions to the fisherman's hut. Again she asked, "Do you understand?"

Bree understood, all right. The minute they could, she and Lil must leave. And they had the food they needed!

"Now, do you remember this prayer?" In her soft clear voice the woman began:

"May God the Father bless us;
May Christ take care of us;
May the Holy Spirit enlighten us
all the days of our life.
The Lord be our Defender
and Keeper of body and soul,
both now and forever,
to the ages of ages."

When Rowena finished, Bree could not see the harbor in front of her. She could not see the mountains. Her tears kept her from seeing anything.

Then her new friend changed the prayer. "May God the Father bless you, Bree. May Christ take care of you, my friend. May the Holy Spirit enlighten you all the days of your life, and may the Lord be your Defender."

Suddenly the gentle Irish voice stopped. With a quick "God go with you, Bree," the Irish woman moved away.

Bree closed up her bag of fish, grasped her pole and line, and picked up her walking stick. Planting the stick in the ground, she used it to pull herself up.

When she set out, Bree walked with a drag to her step and used the stick to keep her balance. Forcing herself to shuffle along, she turned toward the wooded slopes.

Just before she entered the trees, Bree lifted her head. But then her relief died. One thought brought terror to her soul. *What if Mikkel is somewhere in these woods?*

NINE

FISHERMAN'S SECRET

In the darkness before dawn, Mikkel stood on a lower slope of the mountain. For most of the night he had searched the wooded area above the harbor. By now his eyes were used to the dim light.

As he looked down on the harbor, Mikkel noticed the dark outline of an old man sitting on a rock. His shoulders slumped, his head covered by a floppy hat, the fisherman held his pole over the water.

Just then the end of his line jerked down. Moments later, the old man pulled up a good-sized cod, took it off the hook, and put it in the bag next to him. Reaching down, he picked up what seemed to be bait, pushed it onto the hook, and dropped his line into the water again.

Whoever the man was, he certainly knew how to fish. Already he had a bag filled with enough cod for two good-sized meals. But still he kept on.

Mikkel was curious now. Why did one person—one old man, at that—need so much fish? It was too late in the season and too damp for fish to dry well. Finding a rock for himself, Mikkel settled down to watch. But soon his thoughts moved on to other things.

The day before, Mikkel had searched the peninsula around the small settlement called Holmen. Asking questions, he had gone from one Viking house to the next. He had also walked to the king's farm at Alrekstad, but no one had seen Bree and a younger girl. At least no one would admit to seeing them.

Finally Mikkel climbed high in the mountains. During the day he found no one except his own men. At night he had not even seen them.

Now Mikkel thought about what to do next. When dawn came, it would mark the beginning of the third day he and other Vikings searched. How could two young girls—Irish lasses, at that—slip off the face of the earth? How had they gotten away?

Bree couldn't be more than thirteen and the other girl, Lil, might be eight. Nine at most. If they were still alive, how had they managed to survive?

If they were still alive—

Mikkel didn't like to think about that. More than

once during these past days, he had hated himself. Hated the way he baited his men with a reward if they found them. Of course, they would find them. How could they not? All of his men knew how to hunt reindeer. Every one of them set traps for fox and hares. Every man knew how to track and follow, to keep looking until they found their prey.

Mikkel didn't like that word. Bree was no prey. Even if Gunnar thought so, Bree and Lil were not prey. Mikkel only wanted them safe, returned to the ship, and on their way to his home on the Aurland Fjord.

But now a thought accused Mikkel. *That's all you want?*

Mikkel pushed aside the voice and refused to listen. *To see them safe?*

Finally Mikkel had to admit to himself that really wasn't all. As a slave, Bree was valuable. She would bring a good price and help him pay for the ship his father had built for him. More than that, Bree had stolen his bag of silver coins. Only if he recovered them would this voyage make him a wealthy fourteen-year-old.

With all that happened in Ireland, Mikkel hadn't had time to look through his treasure. He only knew that some were Arabic coins brought by traders from far away. No question about it; he had collected a rich horde. True, the coins wouldn't serve as money here in Norway, but Mikkel had big plans for turning them into a valuable profit.

Now the old man took another fish off his line and slipped it into his bag. As Mikkel watched, someone stopped for a moment to talk with the fisherman. Then the old man closed his bag, grasped his pole and line, and used a walking stick to pull himself up.

Mikkel sighed. He was tired of searching. More than once, he had wished things were different and that he and Bree could be friends. Always Mikkel pushed that thought aside. Why would he ever want to be friends with an Irish slave girl?

The old man walked with a drag to his step and used the stout stick to keep his balance. One thing was certain: Judging by the bulge around his waist, he enjoyed his fish. But now his big catch seemed to weigh heavy on his back.

His body a dark outline against the land near the harbor, the old man limped toward the trees. Just before he disappeared, he lifted his head. What was that? Almost an excitement? In the dark Mikkel couldn't be sure.

Well, it would be easy to be excited about such a good catch. Mikkel hadn't felt really excited about anything for quite awhile. Though he'd be rich, it was hard to look forward to what his father would say about the coins Mikkel collected.

The coins he collected? Again Mikkel realized that wasn't quite the right word. Before he returned home, he needed to figure out the best way to tell his father what he'd done.

As the early morning light spread upward, Mikkel saw it first upon the mountains. A thin gold line near the top grew larger, as though inviting him to welcome the day. But Mikkel was still thinking.

If Bree can hide herself so I can't see her, what would she do with a bag of silver coins?

TEN

THE HIDING PLACE

As soon as the trees hid her, Bree felt relieved. Reaching beneath her cloak, she tied the bread and cheese into a better position. Even so, it shifted at least one hundred times before she came to the hideaway high on the mountain.

When Bree crawled into the hollow between the rocks, Lil's smile warmed her.

"Something good happened and something bad," Bree said.

First she pulled out the two loaves of bread and the cheese. Lil's eyes grew round with awe. Both of them knew that God had given them special provision. But then Bree told Lil what Rowena had said.

"Should we go right now?" Lil asked.

"I wish we could." With all her heart Bree wanted to be as far from Mikkel as possible. "But it's especially dangerous to go in daylight. We can't let even one person see us together. We'll leave after dark."

As Bree cleaned fish at the stream, she wondered what to do with all she had caught. Still concerned about finding food on the way, Bree wanted to make the bread and cheese last as long as possible. Then, as she washed the last piece of fish, she felt the coldness of the water.

Near a spot where water spilled over a small ledge, Bree found a hollow and left half of the fish in the cold water. She boiled the other half and brought it to Lil for breakfast.

During the rest of the day, Bree and Lil stayed in their hiding place or left one by one, instead of going out together. Late in the afternoon Bree returned to the fire ring, cooked the last of the fish, and brought it to Lil. By the time they finished their evening meal, the last rays of the sun slanted down upon them.

When Bree went back to put out the cooking fire, she walked over to an opening between clumps of golden birch. Far below, the cluster of houses seemed to be gathered like close friends. From where she stood Bree could see the grass growing from the rooftops. On one roof a goat nibbled at the grass. Bree felt sure that was the house where Rowena lived.

Now the setting sun cast blue and red shadows on the mountains that circled the harbor. The rays of light rested on Mikkel's ship, the *Sea Bird.*

From this height the Viking ship looked like a toy Bree's brother Adam would push around in a puddle of water. Bree felt glad that the ship looked so small. Then she felt the hate in her heart. True, she had always wanted to see what lay beyond the Irish Sea. But when she felt that quest—that deep-down longing that didn't go away —Bree hadn't expected to see the world as a slave.

A *slave?* Not anymore. Not if she could help it.

Ignoring the hard knot inside her, Bree felt glad she could hate Mikkel so much. From the time she was a little girl her mam had told Bree she should learn to forgive. More than once, Bree had stomped her feet and said she would not. She especially would not forgive her brother Dev if he'd done something to tease her.

But now Devin was far away. Over the years she and Dev had learned to make peace between them. Standing there, looking off to the west, Bree felt glad. She also felt glad they'd learned about the courage to win. Bree needed that courage now.

The wood in her cooking fire had nearly burned down to ash, but Bree found a flat stone and dug a hole. Burying the embers, she heaped soil upon them until no spark could flare up.

Then Bree looked down. In the fading light she saw

the ground around the fire ring. In one of the few times Lil left the shelter that day, she had stopped here. Her footprints and Bree's showed clearly. One set looked small and the other set only a bit larger. The prints of their feet would give them away.

Bree sighed. She felt sure that Mikkel and his men had already searched this high. Yet they'd probably come back. They'd notice anything that looked like two people with smaller and larger prints. She could take a fallen branch of leaves, use it like a broom, and sweep away the prints. But someone like Mikkel would suspect unmarked dirt around a fire ring.

As Bree looked for the right branch, she figured out what to do. First, she brushed out the footprints. Then she stood on leaves and rocks outside the circle and decided where to begin.

Carefully she stepped onto the dirt. One at a time, she moved each foot forward, outward, then back, to make her normal print larger. When she finished the first set of prints, Bree grinned. It would work all right. The prints had grown just big enough to belong to the old man she appeared to be.

Enlarging one set of footprints after another, Bree worked her way around the fire ring. At last she felt satisfied and walked off, still making bigger footprints until she reached a path where other people passed by.

Pleased with herself, Bree started to leave. As she glanced far down the mountain, she caught a movement.

With one quick step Bree slipped behind a tree trunk and peered out.

A man stood at the edge of the woods. In the gray light that followed sunset, he was only a silhouette against the lighter sky beyond. But Bree saw that he carried something. A bag, it seemed, and a walking stick that looked more like a stout weapon.

Bending down, the man shoved the stick under a large rock. Then he placed another rock out a few feet and under the stick. Pushing down on the stick, the man lifted the larger rock.

With swift movements he hollowed out a cavity and set the bag into it. Then he lowered the big rock back into place.

Picking up the smaller stone, he set it to one side of the large rock. A short distance away he laid the stick on the ground and covered it with leaves. With a handful of leaves and grass, he smoothed out the ground.

Suddenly the man looked around. Bree ducked back behind the tree and held her breath. When she dared to look again, the man was gone.

Unwilling to take a chance, Bree hid behind the tree for what seemed forever. As she waited, the dusk changed to darkness. Finally, hearing and seeing nothing that made her uneasy, Bree stepped out and started down the mountain.

When she reached the big rock, she set the smaller stone as the man had and shoved the stick under the large rock. With all her strength she pushed down on the stick, but the rock would not move. Several times she tried and finally had to give up.

After swishing away the marks she had made, Bree looked around, and set out for the hollow beneath the oaks. Partway there, she turned back. As soon as she and Lil rested a bit, they would flee under the cover of darkness. At the fire ring Bree picked up the soapstone pot, and took it with her.

Tired as she was, she took a roundabout way to the hiding place. Often she glanced over her shoulder. Once she wondered if she saw a shadow that moved out of sight. Bree stopped and waited, but all was still. Bree decided she had imagined things.

When she reached their hideaway, Lil was sleeping. Lying down, Bree told herself she'd rest for only a few minutes. Instead, she fell asleep.

Bree woke to the smell of danger. *The smell of danger?* She wasn't sure she knew what that was. She only knew they had to get moving. Like a fire burning in her bones, she felt the warning. Somehow, someway, someone had discovered their hiding place.

Instantly alert, Bree pulled on her tunic and shoes. When she started moving around, she discovered Lil was already awake.

"What is it?" Lil's voice was so soft that her whisper barely reached Bree.

"You know it too?" Bree asked. "What's wrong?"

"I don't know. I only know we need to leave."

Bree collected the soapstone pot, set the cheese inside, and rolled that and the bread into her blanket. With Nola's last strips of leather she tied the bundle to her back. A moment later Lil was also ready.

As they left the hollow in the rocks, Bree remembered. Once again they must hide their footprints.

The ground around their shelter was more firm than when they came, but Bree took the lead and walked on rock, grass, or leaves wherever she could. Though the night wind was cold, the sky was clear, and the waning moon rode high. Bree felt grateful for its light.

As clearly as if Rowena spoke from behind, Bree remembered the directions she had given. Turning away from the harbor, Bree set her face toward the mountain on which she and Lil stood.

Already they were so high that they walked on nearly level ground. Here where there were fewer trees, it was not hard to see the way. For some time they walked straight ahead, simply looking for rocky ground that would hide their footprints. Pushing aside her uneasy feelings Bree tried to remember whatever she could about the land they crossed.

Strangely enough, now that they had set out, she felt something else. Whatever it was that sent them forth, they were ahead of it. The important thing seemed to be that they simply find a new hiding place. But where?

"Set your direction and keep going around things as needed," Rowena had said. But how could Bree know her direction for a place she had never been?

As they reached an open space, Bree stopped. "Let's pray," she told Lil. "Let's ask God to help us know what to do."

When they finished praying, Bree stood there waiting. Then, like a reminder from deep inside, she remembered Rowena's words. "Wherever you go, watch the stars," the Irish woman had said, as if knowing Bree would leave at night.

Bree's sister Keely had always been the one who liked the stars. Even as a baby she pointed up at the sky and clapped her hands. But Bree could at least recognize the North Star. Now she used it to keep going in one direction.

Sometimes she and Lil walked around a black ridge of rocks. Sometimes they found the way so steep that they crawled over rocks two, three, or four feet high. But then they came to a place that seemed impossible to pass.

"Walk until you can't walk any farther," Rowena had told them. Now Bree knew what she meant. Against the night sky the rock was so dark, so high, and so straight up and down that it seemed like a wall with no way around.

"What should we do? Lil whispered.

Bree shrugged and looked back.

"Do you think someone followed us?"

Bree shook her head. But in the darkness how could she be sure?

ELEVEN

THE FOUR GUARDS

When Mikkel returned to his tent after another nighttime search, he felt angry. He not only wanted to sail for home, he *needed* to leave before bad weather set in. Yet he was unwilling to go on until he found Bree and recovered his coins. How could two Irish lasses manage to escape all the Vikings who searched for them?

The more Mikkel thought about it, the more upset he became. Instead of going to bed, he went for a walk. He sat down along the shore, away from the tents.

The night was clear, and the light of the moon rested on trees and cast shadows across the mountains. At first Mikkel listened to the lap of waves against the shore. Then, through the open flaps of a tent, he saw a tall, slender man stand up. A coil of rope hung over Gunnar's shoulder. The handle of his sword glinted in the moonlight.

As Mikkel sat without moving, another man followed Gunnar. Shorter than any other Viking, the second man had to be Alf. Then a third and a fourth man joined the others. The four guards who allowed Bree and Lil to escape!

Mikkel felt sure he knew where they were going. Somehow the men had discovered Bree's hiding place. No doubt they had joined forces so they could all get the reward of double wages. Mikkel felt for his knife, pushed it deeper into its sheath, and set out after them.

The four Vikings were easy to follow. Though walking quietly, they made no attempt to hide their movements. Along the shore they hurried, then into the trees at the end of the harbor. When they disappeared, Mikkel moved quickly to close the distance between them. Even when they started up the steep side of the mountain, he stayed not far behind.

Wherever the men were going, they knew the exact place and were in full agreement on what to do. That's what bothered Mikkel the most.

Near a large boulder far up the mountain the four men split up. Two slipped away and disappeared into the darkness of higher ground. The remaining two crept quietly forward, one on either side of the boulder. Drawing close to a large oak, Gunnar slipped under the outermost branches. Alf stood at the other end.

Moving like a shadow from tree to tree, Mikkel drew close. As he waited, he heard the shrill *caw, caw, caw,* of a crow.

Moments later, a second crow answered. When Mikkel heard a third and a fourth, he knew it was a signal. In that moment Gunnar disappeared behind the boulder.

Running without sound, Mikkel drew close. Staying in the shadow of trees, he climbed higher until he looked down on the place where the men disappeared. Inside the hollow behind the boulder, the four of them stood looking around. But the moonlight that reached even there showed one thing. Except for the men, the hollow between the rocks was empty.

Pulling out his sword, Gunnar slashed at the trunk of a large tree. An angry voice joined Gunnar's, then a third and a fourth man spoke up, as they argued among themselves.

Though he couldn't hear their words, Mikkel listened to their anger and knew that Bree and Lil were gone. Relief washed over him like a wave rushing toward shore.

Silently he edged back and crept away. His men must not know he had followed them, but now Mikkel felt even more desperate. His instincts were right. He must find Bree and Lil before the men did.

As Mikkel walked back to his ship, he passed the place where the old man had fished. For a moment

Mikkel stood there, wishing his life could be as simple as catching a mess of fish.

As clearly as if he still saw it, Mikkel remembered how the man pulled himself up, using a stout stick for balance. The walk had been perfect, an old man's gait with a shuffle that was real. Though carrying a weight on his back, he moved forward by leaning on his stick. But at that last moment—

What was it? What changed?

The man lifted his head.

So, a man lifted his head, and you wonder if it was Bree?

Like an accusing voice, the thought struck him. Not even Bree could fool him that much. *It isn't possible. I couldn't look at her and not see her.*

But where is she?

Filled with despair, Mikkel dropped down on the rock where the old man had sat. Like the fisherman, he peered down into the water. As the sun rose above the water, Mikkel saw his reflection. Strange.

All summer he had been at sea. Until now he had no idea how hard his face had become. But Mikkel felt sure it was not just time that had aged him. He hadn't been gone from home that long. Nor could the wind and sun change him that much. Deep in his heart Mikkel knew it was something more—the choices he had made. The choices he was starting to hate.

"I will protect you," he had told Bree soon after his

men captured her. "I will protect you, but you must obey me."

Now Mikkel saw her wide brown eyes and the innocent look Bree turned on at a moment's notice. More than once, he had thought she was getting used to the idea of being a slave. Instead, in all the ways that he underestimated Bree, she had gotten the best of him.

First, in freeing her brother Devin. Next, in her escape from the ship. Then, in stealing his coins and managing to hide. And now, in yet another escape.

Mikkel felt foolish, but he was no fool. Not only would he find her, but he would make her pay for every way she'd shown her independence, for every time she'd figured out a way to win. He'd make her sorry for every moment she showed spirit.

Spirit. Suddenly Mikkel knew he needed to be honest with himself. He'd make Bree regret every way she showed *courage.*

In that moment Mikkel saw deep inside himself. He saw all that he didn't want to admit. A bottomless hole that nothing seemed to fill. And he wanted to punish Bree for the very courage that he himself lacked.

Climb a mast in a storm? Lead a group of men where he wanted to go? Raid and steal? No problem. If he kept choosing to steal, he would become a wealthy man.

But courage? Real courage? The kind of courage that prodded Bree to stand up for what she believed? The kind of courage that kept her looking out for others beside herself?

Much as he hated to admit it, Mikkel knew that kind of courage was missing from his life.

Thinking about it, he felt angry again. Then there was something he knew. If he was ever going to get Bree and his silver coins back, he needed to put aside his anger and think. Deliberately, Mikkel told himself to keep his mind on what he needed to know.

When the idea came, it surprised even him.

For the first time Mikkel started to wonder how Bree would think. What would she do? Mikkel had absolutely no idea. He couldn't even imagine himself being Bree.

As the impossibility of it overwhelmed him, Mikkel began praying to his favorite god. But no answer came, and Mikkel did not understand what to do. He felt as if he was praying to a wall of stones as big as these mountains. Besides, when Mikkel and the other Vikings really needed Thor during the storm, he didn't answer.

Maybe he doesn't want to show me where Bree is. Bree says she has her own God. Maybe the gods of my land don't like that she's here. In the storm—

Mikkel didn't like thinking about that storm. When the mast dipped toward the waves, he had nearly lost his life. Since then he'd held a fear of the water he'd never known before.

But Bree—when he'd shouted at her to pray to Thor,

she'd refused. Instead, Bree and the other Irish had asked their God to still the storm. And He had.

Mikkel couldn't understand that. All his life he'd heard only about his own gods—the gods that his father and mother worshiped—the gods their whole village worshiped. How could there be another God more powerful than the ones he and his family knew?

Yet now Mikkel was desperate. Turning, he glanced around to make sure no one was close by. When he saw the beach was empty, he closed his eyes the way he had seen Bree do on the ship. Facing the water, he began praying.

"I don't know who You are so I'll call You 'Bree's God.' And I don't need You for myself. I have my own gods, and they're stronger than You. But Bree makes You sound like You're important. Since she thinks that, maybe You want to take care of her. If You care about Bree, You'd better help me find her before someone else does."

When Mikkel opened his eyes, nothing seemed to have changed. Then, as a morning mist rose above the water, he felt still deep inside. He had looked upon Bree. He had watched her pull fish after fish from this water. But because of that one moment when she lifted her head, Mikkel knew.

The old man is Bree.

TWELVE

DUBLIN DANGER

When Devin and Jeremy reached the river Liffey, they stood on the bank and looked across to the city of Dublin. Named *Dubhlinn* or "black pool" from the dark color of the water, the river was indeed dark. But to Devin it also looked clear. The water reflected the late afternoon light.

Here the river Poodle joined the wide lower part of the Liffey where its current met the tides of the Irish Sea. Nearly surrounded by water, Dublin was the first true town in Ireland. It was also an independent Norse kingdom—a trade center established by Vikings from the North Atlantic.

A high earth embankment formed a circle around

Dublin. On top of that embankment, a tall fence of timber poles added another defensive barrier.

Jeremy stared at the high wall. "Now what do we do?" he asked.

"It looks like a fort, doesn't it?" As much as Devin wanted to find a way to help Bree, he really didn't want to enter the city. But then Devin saw the openings in the earth and timber walls. At least there was more than one place to get in and out if needed.

"Maybe we could work for a pair of shoes," Jeremy said.

Devin grinned. Once again, Jeremy was trying to take care of him. Devin wasn't used to that, for he had always been the one to watch out for Bree and his younger sisters and brother. But Devin had to admit that shoes would be mighty fine. One of his toes was bleeding from the most recent cut.

"A shoemaker. A cobbler," he said, and in that moment Devin remembered. "That's who my father trusts. He trades with a Norseman—a Viking from the North Atlantic. But I still can't remember his name."

Maybe if he and Jeremy walked up and down the streets, they would see something to help him remember. But first, they needed to cross the river.

When they walked down next to the water, a man in a small rowboat called to them. "Be you wanting a way across?"

Devin nodded. "Are you a ferry, then? We don't have the money."

"Ah, such fine lads as you. Just wait and I'll take you with another crossin'."

Before long, a young gentleman wanted to go over. When the ferryman waved to them, Devin and Jeremy tucked themselves into one end of the boat.

At the far side of the river, no one seemed to notice as they climbed the steps and passed through the opening into the city. For a moment Devin stood there, looking around.

A wide path led straight ahead, and from there other streets led out. Along those streets, smaller stakes were driven into the ground as a fence around every house. And here, as at home, all the roofs were made of straw thatch.

"This is a Viking city?" Jeremy asked. "They build like us."

Devin glanced at the sun. Moment by moment it was edging its way down in the west. If they wanted to find a shopkeeper, they needed to do it soon.

As Devin started walking again, the noise of the city surrounded him. Strolling up and down the street, men called out, "Fish for sale! Fish for sale!" Carts rumbled past. Chickens squawked and sheep bleated. After being in the quiet countryside, Devin felt overwhelmed by noise. He wanted only to find the cobbler and leave as quickly as he could.

Speaking in Norse, the trade language his father had taught him, Devin started asking directions. In a city of 10,000 people there was more than one cobbler. Devin stood still, looking around and trying to remember the name of his father's friend.

In the midst of all the noise he tried to pray, tried to ask for help. But still he felt as if a giant wall—a wall higher than the one around Dublin—had gone up between him and God.

Always his friends had known Devin as someone who was strong in whatever he did. More often than not, Devin won in whatever he took on. But now Devin knew there was something that could keep him from winning. How could he go into this city of Vikings and ask for help when he hated every Viking he knew?

"What's wrong?" Jeremy asked when Devin did not move on.

"I'm scared," Devin whispered. "I'm scared of every person in this city." *How can Bree stand it, being surrounded by Vikings?*

"Oh, Dev, you're not scared," Jeremy said.

"I am."

"What makes you scared?"

And then Devin knew. The hate in his heart made him weak. But how could he not hate the men who had taken Bree and Keely away?

Once more he started walking. This time he asked for

the names of cobblers and heard one he recognized. "It's Bjorn!" he said. "That's who it is." A few minutes later, Devin and Jeremy found his shop.

When Devin opened the door, the man working at a shoemaker's bench looked up.

"Are you Bjorn?" Devin asked.

"That I am." The man smiled.

"I need a pair of shoes," Devin began. "I don't have money, but if you allow Jeremy"—Devin turned to his friend—"if you allow Jeremy and me to work, we'll pay for them."

"And what kind of shoes would you like?"

Devin took out the pair he had carried for the last three days. Even though he had taken them off, Devin suspected that Red Shirt had followed them. Perhaps he guessed that Devin and Jeremy headed for Dublin.

"Ah, these are not hard to make," Bjorn said when he saw Devin's shoe. "It will take me no time at all. But where are you from?"

When Devin told him, the man laid down his tools and listened. "From Glendalough, you said?" And that was all, until the man asked Devin's name.

"Your father, lad?"

"Aidan O'Toole."

"And it's your sister you lost?"

"Two sisters. Keely and Bree."

"And do you know the name of the man who led the raid?"

"His name is Mikkel." Suddenly the hate bottled up inside Devin spilled out. Like a river leaving its banks, he spit Mikkel's name across the room. And with it, he spit the name of Mikkel's father. "A mighty chieftain he is. Sigurd, a mighty chieftain of Aurland, Norway."

Then, to Devin's great embarrassment, he began to weep. Great, long, rasping sobs tore from him. Sobs that broke like a dam from his stored-up hatred. Sobs that shook every part of his body.

To Devin's surprise the cobbler got up from his workbench and stretched his long arms around him. Like a young boy Devin stood without moving, knowing only that he needed the comfort of those arms.

When at last Devin stopped weeping, the cobbler stepped back. "I ask your forgiveness," Bjorn said.

His kindness brought a fresh torrent of tears. In the long, terrible days since the raid, Devin had decided that all Vikings were like Mikkel.

"You ask my forgiveness?" Devin asked when he could speak. "But it wasn't you. It was Mikkel who did it. Mikkel, son of Sigurd."

"Of the Aurland Fjord. His father is indeed a mighty chieftain. He is a good man."

Devin stared at Bjorn and backed away. "You know Mikkel's father?" Pushing Jeremy behind him, Devin wanted only to protect the boy from the shoemaker.

But Bjorn spoke quickly. "Never fear. Mikkel's father is a worthy man. I have traded with him for many years."

"But Mikkel?"

"His father will weep to know what Mikkel has done. He has dishonored the family name. Mikkel has not only hurt your family; he has hurt me. When he came to sell his goods—the skins gathered by the men of the Aurland Fjord—I gave him fair payment. But after he was gone, I found he had taken not only what he earned, but also a bag of silver coins."

"He stole from you?"

"Some of the coins are Arabic. Some from Constantinople. Before I became a cobbler I sailed all over the world. The coins have great value. But—"

The Norwegian held up his hand. "They have no value when compared to your sisters Keely and Bree. For what happened to them I ask your forgiveness."

Once again Devin started to weep. Once again the large man put his arms around him and patted him on the back.

"I ask your forgiveness for Mikkel," Bjorn said. "I ask your forgiveness for whoever took Keely away."

When he could weep no more, Devin finally understood. Forgiving Mikkel did not mean saying that what he did was right. Instead, forgiveness gave Devin a way to stop hating and go on.

As he lifted his head, the cobbler's arms fell away. Reaching out, Devin took Jeremy's hand and looked up into Bjorn's face. In that moment Devin knew what to do.

"You stand for your countrymen," he told the shoemaker. "You stand for cruel men and the boy named Mikkel. Jeremy and I stand for the Irish. For all the Irish the Vikings have hurt. And we forgive you."

For a moment the tall man stood without moving. Then he, too, began to weep.

"Come, lads," he said at last. "You see how Irish I have become, calling you 'lads'? Would you like a hot meal? A place to sleep? My good wife will feed you Irish stew and give you a bed."

It took only a minute for the cobbler to close up his shop. As Bjorn led them down the street, bells began to ring.

Bells? Devin wondered if he was hearing things. But Bjorn smiled.

"Church bells. Don't you know? Dublin is known as the city rich in bells."

THIRTEEN

LONESOME FOR HOME

In the shadow of the rock Bree and Lil spread out their blankets and slept the rest of the night. With the dawn of a new day Bree sliced bread and cheese and found water. Then she remembered more of Rowena's words. "When you come to a high wall, go left."

To Bree's surprise, she and Lil were able to walk around the high rock and find a way beyond. But an hour later, Lil started to cough.

In the beginning it sounded like a tickle in the throat, and Bree wondered if Lil felt nervous about another escape.

"Are you afraid?" Bree asked, and Lil shook her head. Their hope of getting away from the Vikings seemed more possible all the time.

Once they needed to circle a lake. Often they jumped across a small stream. But soft ground nearly fooled Bree. She was used to bog in Ireland, but she didn't expect it here. When she came to a flat stretch of land, Bree started across. Suddenly her feet sank into mushy soil.

Instantly she leaped to a rock. From there she backed away to solid ground. But once again they lost time while circling around a large area instead of going across.

Before long, Lil's hack changed into a deeper cough. Listening, Bree told herself it couldn't possibly be serious. God had taken them through one hard time after another —always providing shelter, clothes, and food. He had even hidden them away from the Vikings. How could God bring them this far and then let them fail?

When they stopped for their noon meal, Bree looked at the food and felt concerned. Here where there were mountain streams she could start fishing again. But they needed to keep moving. If they were careful, they had enough bread for three more days. Enough cheese for two.

It took one second for Bree to decide. She would give Lil bread and cheese, but skip eating herself. She'd say she wasn't hungry.

But Bree's stomach growled in the midst of her lie. Lil giggled. "You aren't hungry? Let's split what you're giving me instead."

When they set out again, Bree stopped several times

to give the younger girl time to rest. Always it was Lil who said, "Let's keep going." Just the same, Bree was not fooled. They needed to find a shelter.

By now they were far enough from Mikkel's ship that Bree felt safe about asking for help. But here, high in the mountains, she found no farmer's house, no door on which to knock. And if she had figured distances right, they were still a two-day walk from the fisherman's hut.

Bree could think of only one thing. *What will I do if Lil gets really sick?*

All day Lil kept saying she was fine, but by mid-afternoon Bree knew she was having trouble keeping up. "We're going to stop," Bree told her. "You need to rest."

"If we keep walking—" A cough cut off Lil's words.

Bree shook her head. "When you feel better, we'll go on."

They were crossing another rocky stretch of ground. Here and there were large boulders, sometimes with high shelves. If only she could find the right one—

Taking Lil's bundle, Bree opened the reindeer hide and spread it out in the shadow of a rock. "Lie down," Bree told her. "I'll come back for you."

When Bree first saw the right spot, she looked at it without understanding the possibilities. She had hoped for a cave or a shelter under some trees. But then she walked out on a wide, flat ledge.

Not far away, a stream tumbled over rocks. Fresh

water! And just below where Bree stood was a wide, fairly level stretch of rock.

Climbing down, Bree found that the ledge on which she had stood was an overhang with a rock wall. Shaped like a U, the tucked-away spot would shelter them from wind on three sides. And on the fourth? If it got too cold, Bree would find a way to protect them from the west wind.

The west wind. Bree thought about it. When she could, she'd face into the wind and dream of the misty fields of Ireland.

And Lil will get well! Bree knew it. They would travel on, find the fisherman's hut along the shore, and get passage to Ireland. If only she could find her sister Keely first. *After all these years, what would it be like to see Keely again?*

Since escaping the Viking ship, Bree had thought little about anything except how to survive. Now she dared to dream about her new quest—being home with her family again. What would it be like to walk up to her family's cottage? To open the door and walk in? Already Bree could feel their arms around her.

But then she remembered. Until she left Mikkel far behind she was still a slave. A slave accused of stealing a bag of silver coins. And the penalty for that was death.

When Bree returned to Lil, the eight-year-old was sleeping. The knitted cap had slipped up, no longer covering her black hair and eyebrows. Her face looked pale, and Bree saw the shadows beneath her eyes.

Instantly all of Bree's dreams vanished. She couldn't push away her frightened questions. Had she done the right thing, bringing Lil here? For Lil to be a slave of the Vikings was unthinkable. But now? What would happen to Lil? And when would winter come in these mountains?

When Lil opened her eyes, Bree did her best to keep her voice calm. "I've found a new home for us," she said.

As Lil stood up, she stumbled, and Bree knew Lil had been hiding her weakness. Dropping their bundles, Bree offered a shoulder and arm to help her. When they reached the sheltered place, Lil sank to her knees and lay down on the rock warmed by the sun.

Bree went back to pick up their bundles. As she started to leave again, she looked down. Her concern about Lil was making her careless.

Marks in the earth showed where Lil had slept. Other marks told anyone who searched that they had set down bundles. The soil was soft, leaving unmistakable evidence that they had passed that way.

Bree found dried grass and smoothed the ground. Quickly she spread fallen leaves and grass over the soil. Then, watching carefully for footprints or other marks, Bree hurried back to Lil. When she reached their new hiding place, Lil was sleeping again.

Through the long hours of the night Lil coughed. Bree lay awake, wondering what to do. By morning Lil was no better. Instead, her face looked flushed. When

Bree felt Lil's forehead, she knew the younger girl had a fever.

A hard knot of worry formed in Bree's stomach. Taking the soapstone pot, Bree got water from the stream, then put a cold cloth on Lil's forehead. All day long Bree kept changing the cloth, trying to bring down Lil's temperature. In between, Bree caught fish and collected wood. And all the time her worry grew.

When the rattle began in Lil's chest, Bree's worry changed to overwhelming fear. "It's not fair!" she cried out to God. "I can't even ask my mam what to do!"

Bree had watched her mother take care of Devin when he was very ill. But could she possibly remember?

In the nearby stream Bree again filled the soapstone pot with water. Now she had no choice but to start a fire. Bree set the wood as close to the overhanging rock as she could and hoped that if Mikkel followed, he would not see the flame.

When the water in the pot grew warm, Bree dipped a cloth in it and squeezed it out. As she put the warm cloth over Lil's chest, the eight-year-old opened her eyes and looked up.

For a moment Lil's eyes were clear, and Bree felt relieved. Maybe Lil was past the worst. Maybe she would get well now. And when Lil spoke, everything seemed right again. But then she asked, "Are you wondering if you should have brought me with?"

Inside Bree, something snapped. Since leaving the Viking ship, she had often wondered just that. With Lil so sick, Bree felt even more guilty.

But now Lil said, "Thanks for taking me, Bree."

Her voice was weak, and Bree leaned closer to hear. On Lil's second try Bree caught it. "If I die—"

"No!" Bree cried. "You aren't going to die!"

"If I die, remember that I'm home."

"Home? In Ireland?" Bree whispered, terrified.

Lil barely moved her head, but Bree knew she was trying to get her to understand.

"Home in heaven. Remember how much I love Jesus."

Coughing wracked Lil's body, and she tried to raise herself up. Bree slipped her arm behind Lil's back and helped her to a sitting position. Again Lil's cough rattled in her chest.

When it stopped, Lil lay back. Her voice was raspy and she could barely speak. "You know, and I know that Jesus died on the cross for us. Men took Him like a slave—"

Bree tried to help. "And you don't like being a slave."

"But Jesus *let* the soldiers take Him," Lil said. "He didn't have to die, but He did. He died for you. He died for me." When Lil put her hand on her chest, she started coughing again.

Bree drew a deep breath. What Lil wanted to tell her was important, but Bree felt so scared she didn't want to hear another word. She only wanted this talk about death to end. She wanted Lil to get well.

Then Bree knew that Lil would not stop until she was sure Bree understood what she was saying. As Bree tried to help, her voice was gentle. "Jesus made the most important choice in the entire world. He died for all of us."

Suddenly Lil relaxed and lay back. "If I die, remember that I've asked Him to forgive my sin. To be my Savior. And He is."

Lil's voice was stronger now. Reaching up, she pointed to the sky and made the sign of the cross in the air above her.

But then Lil closed her eyes. Her voice was weak again. "I'm lonesome for home."

Bree understood that. She, too, was lonesome for home, but for her it meant Ireland.

For a long time she sat next to Lil, holding her hand. As the water started to boil, the stream of vapor drifted toward them. The gentle mist hung about Lil's face, and Bree did not move.

As her young friend dozed off, Bree prayed harder than she had ever prayed in her life.

FOURTEEN

BREE'S GOD

When Mikkel felt sure that his four men were gone, he climbed back up the mountain. By now he was so tired of climbing that he wished he had never heard of a girl named Bree.

This time he took a different way. When he saw the fire ring, he knew Bree must have used it without leaving her footprints. When he came to the hollow in the rocks, the morning sunlight sifted down between the trees. Standing there, he looked at a place swept clean of any sign except those left by his own men.

And there he understood something new about Bree. She would leave no mark at a place she had been—no sign that she had passed by. No sign, except in someone's heart.

More than ever before, Mikkel felt afraid for her. What should he do?

Somehow he must track Bree and Lil with every skill he knew from hunting reindeer, hares, and fox. So far the girls had not left one footprint. Even around the stream there had been no trace of their steps. And the fire? Footprints of others—men, it appeared, with larger feet. But no footprints that would fit two girls.

Not only had Bree trained herself; she had trained Lil. What's more, he had seen Bree carry away his bag of coins. And he thought she'd eaten a lot of fish! But would she continue to use that disguise? Mikkel had no way of knowing.

And Lil? He could only believe that she would be with Bree.

Upset now at what seemed to be an impossible task, Mikkel started walking. At an open spot between birch trees, he looked out on the valley. As the sun shone above the mountains in the east, golden rays lit other peaks. Far below, blue water sparkled like a jewel. Mikkel felt glad to be in Norway again. But he also felt fear.

Or was it a warning? Whichever it was, he had to find Bree first.

Sitting down on the side of the mountain, Mikkel studied the land before him. From mountain to mountain his gaze went. Up and down the steep slopes he watched for any sign of life. But with his newfound knowledge about Bree, Mikkel had no doubt that in daylight, she and Lil were safely hidden away. Where would they go?

Again Mikkel felt the warning. How much time did he have? How did Gunnar and Alf know where to look when he didn't? It frightened Mikkel.

At the small settlement called Holmen his ship—his *Sea Bird*—was drawn up on shore. Beyond that was the passage through the western islands to the Norwegian Sea. At the other end of the harbor, a large body of water lay like a giant bowl near the king's farm named Alrekstad.

In that moment there was something Mikkel knew. From the start Bree had prepared to leave this place. That's what all the fishing was about. She had hauled in one after another. What would two girls do with that many fish?

Now that he no longer underestimated Bree's skills, Mikkel took a guess. Bree didn't know the air was too damp to dry fish this time of year. She'd try to fill a bag with dried fish and set out over the mountains. And if she somehow learned a place to go—

Thinking about it, Mikkel knew there were two good possibilities.

If Bree had come this way, she, too, would have looked down upon the harbor. The water between would keep her from crossing to the mountains on the other side. She would need to walk around behind the king's farm.

Would she take that risk? Mikkel doubted it.

Suddenly Mikkel laughed aloud. For the first time he thought he understood what Bree would do. She would take the second and easiest possibility. Turning toward the mountain on which he stood, Mikkel started climbing.

Soon he found it wasn't as easy to follow Bree and Lil as he'd hoped. Once again he discovered no tracks. No broken branches. No remains of a fire.

Once again Bree had fooled him. He thought sure he had chosen the right way, but if he had, where was she?

By mid afternoon of the second day, Mikkel felt ready to give up. Turning, he started back to the hollow where Bree and Lil had hid. Angry now about all the time he had wasted, Mikkel barely watched where he was going. Suddenly he stepped into boggy ground.

And that was where Mikkel saw the footprints. The right foot, then the left. Footprints of a size that could be Bree's. Then nothing.

Mikkel stared at the prints, then looked for a rock. Yes, there it was. A rock just the right distance away for Bree to step out. Beyond that, more rocky ground.

Mikkel grinned. *Bree made a mistake. I'll find her yet!*

He had only one clue. The direction her feet pointed before she knew it was soft ground. Setting out again, Mikkel went around the boggy area but kept the direction.

After walking some distance, he started looking for a place to stop. Darkness would soon be upon him and he could stumble into a dangerous chasm. In the morning he would catch up and take those Irish lasses back to the ship.

The *Sea Bird.* His ship.

In spite of Bree's escape, Mikkel still felt proud of all that he had accomplished and proud of the wealth he was bringing home.

But then Mikkel's thoughts grew hard. As though his father stood before him, Mikkel saw Sigurd, the mighty chieftain of the Aurland Fjord. With a strong face and solid chin, he had deep blue eyes with a stern look that Mikkel dreaded.

As the youngest son of the family, Mikkel would not inherit land. Yet Mikkel loved the sea as much as he loved the land. When his father had said he would build him a ship, Mikkel felt only the desire to succeed. If he brought a good return on his father's investment, he could pay off the ship. With more successful trips—more raids to glean wealth from foreign soil—he, Mikkel, would build his fame.

As the dusk gathered around him, Mikkel looked off to the horizon and smiled. He would allow nothing to hinder his plans. Someday those plans would reach far beyond the Norwegian Sea—far beyond the Atlantic Ocean. *For I will be a wealthy man.*

Then in the fading light Mikkel saw what seemed to be a flame in the distance. As the light flickered and nearly disappeared from view, he wondered if he was seeing things. Heading that way, Mikkel followed the light.

The fire was built under an overhang that hid most of the flames from anyone coming from his direction. Looking around, Mikkel decided on the best way to draw close, and he crept forward without a sound.

What he saw brought him up short. The old man was there, without an eye patch. He still wore the dirty clothes and floppy hat that covered most of his hair. But it was Bree's small clean hands that gave her away. Even on the ship she somehow managed to look clean.

Quietly Mikkel sat down with his back against a large stone. After his long search, he should feel glad to find Bree. Instead, he felt sorry that she had lost.

Mikkel pushed the thought away, hating himself for it. In that moment he remembered. Where was Lil?

Blankets lay close to the rock wall and out of the wind. Was Lil huddled inside them? This time of night she should have been up and around. Was something wrong?

For a time Mikkel watched. Whatever Bree had done with his bag of coins, she no longer wore it around her waist. At least she looked a good deal thinner. Sliding her arm under Lil's shoulder, Bree helped her drink from a soapstone pot.

Then Bree walked to the nearby stream, put some cloths in the cold water, and wrung them out. Then she filled the pot with water, carried it back to the shelter, and set it over the fire.

All evening long, Mikkel watched Bree take care of Lil. Soon he realized there truly was something wrong. Bree was on her knees, weeping as if her heart would break.

For the first time doubt crept into Mikkel's mind. Could someone who cared that much about a young girl really steal a bag of coins? But how could it be anyone else? Vikings had searched all the other Irish and their possessions as well. If not Bree, who could it be?

Could it possibly be Gunnar? But Gunnar knew the penalty for theft.

Then, as Mikkel watched, Bree took off her old hat and looked up. In that instant she stopped weeping and her face shone. The light of the fire faded in the light that surrounded Bree.

Suddenly Mikkel fell to his knees. Whatever the light was, it had to be Bree's God.

FIFTEEN

SHADOW IN THE FOG

Sometime after dark, Bree dipped the cloth in warm water, squeezed it out, and put it on Lil's chest. Pushing back Lil's hair, Bree felt her forehead. Her skin was cool.

Filled with panic, Bree leaned close to listen to Lil's breathing. Quiet and even it was, with no rattle in her chest. Lil's temperature had broken!

Bree dropped to her knees. *She will get well!*

Bree wanted to shout it to the world. *Lil will get well!*

But then Bree began to cry. So relieved that she could not stop, Bree sobbed until she could weep no more.

When at last she sat up, Bree reached out again and touched Lil's forehead. Even now it seemed impossible that her temperature was really gone.

As Lil slept on, Bree moved closer to the fire. Here, where she could still take care of her friend, Bree wanted to be alone with God.

At first Bree's gratitude tumbled from her. Like a stream spilling over with water, she could not thank God enough. For hours and days she had felt overwhelmed by fear. Now her thanks and praise swept everything else away.

In the stillness of the night around her, Bree waited and listened. Not far away, the water in the stream rippled over rocks. A breeze whispered in the pines, and Bree felt peace. Closing her eyes, she rested.

Then she heard it. *Briana.*

Bree stirred.

Briana.

Was Lil asking for her? She always called her Bree.

Briana, came the voice again.

Only her parents and Brother Cronan called her Briana. When Bree opened her eyes, a white light surrounded her. A light? Had the moon come out from under the clouds?

But then Bree knew that no moon could be this bright. On her knees again, she looked up. From the center of the light she sensed a voice. Or was it a Bible verse she learned long ago?

I have called you to be a light to the nations.

For a moment longer the light rested upon her, giving peace. Then as the light faded, the words still echoed in Bree's heart.

A light to the nations? What did that mean?

For a long time Bree knelt there, praying. Finally she knew. Whatever it meant, God would show her in the time ahead.

In the morning Bree woke to a milky white world. During the night, a thick wall of fog had rolled in from the sea. Like a wet blanket it hung in the air, shutting out the world. But Bree was still thinking about the words she had heard the night before.

I have called you to be a light to the nations.

"Thank You, Lord," Bree whispered. Without doubt she knew those words were God's promise to her.

The night before, Bree hadn't known what that meant. This morning she still wasn't sure. Now she started thinking about all the things it *could* mean.

Since their escape, God had helped her and Lil in countless ways. Surely that meant they would reach the freedom they wanted. Hadn't good St. Patrick escaped slavery before returning to Ireland as a missionary?

Soon Bree felt sure that she knew what God planned. After all, if she *didn't* get completely away, how could she be a light to the nations?

As Bree thought about it, hope filled her heart. She and Lil would earn their way back to Ireland. The minute Lil was strong enough, they'd set out again. No matter how long it took, they'd find the hut along the sea. The fisherman would take them to Ireland.

Full of plans, Bree reached out to touch Lil's forehead. The younger girl still felt cool. Her breathing sounded clear and good. But here, even under the overhang, the air felt wet and cold. During the night the fire had burned low.

Bree jumped up, slipped on her shoes, and set out to find wood. Already she had picked up all the windfalls nearby. As Lil's illness grew worse, Bree had been afraid to leave her. Now she had no choice. They would soon be out of wood.

Climbing down between the rocks next to their shelter, Bree started away from the area she knew best. In spite of the thick fog, she walked fast, searching with each step for branches on the ground.

At first Bree could see far enough to know where she was going. Then the fog became so thick that it felt like a cold blanket around her. Before long, Bree could not see beyond the length of her arms.

From the time she was a little girl Bree had known the dangers of fog. In the Wicklow Mountains she sat down wherever she was and waited for the sun and wind to snatch a thick cloud away. But now Bree thought of Lil. How would she feel if she woke to find Bree gone?

Suddenly Bree realized it was more important to get back than to find wood. Turning around, she climbed over a rock and tried to hurry. Instead, she slipped on moss. As she crashed down, Bree started sliding. To her relief she came up against a large stone.

The jolt to her body hurt, but Bree picked herself up and went on. Yet now she felt confused. Covered by fog, the sun gave an eerie light. Bree could find no landmarks, no sense of direction. From which way had she come? Where was she going? Bree only knew that her world seemed strangely empty.

Then she heard a sound. Was someone there with her after all? Had Lil gotten up and started walking around?

Bree stopped, peered into the fog, and listened. What was it?

In the damp air every sound changed. The world seemed hollow. Who's there? she wondered. Someone I can't see?

As Bree wondered what to do, a shadow slipped into the wall of fog in front of her. The shadow stood without moving. Milky light fell on windblown blond hair.

Then the shadow took shape as a person with strong shoulders and arms. The tall lad stood with head lifted and feet apart, blocking her way.

Ready to run, Bree whirled around. Suddenly a hand grabbed her arm and hung on. In that instant Bree saw the ground drop away. Two feet beyond where she stood, the chasm was so deep that fog hid the bottom.

Bree's heart thudded. She had nearly dropped off a straight-up-and-down rock. How far would she have fallen? Hundreds of feet? Bree didn't know.

When she turned to face Mikkel, he released her arm, but his face was angry. He had chosen his spot well. How he had gotten there, Bree had no idea. How he managed to get around, then ahead of her, she could not fathom. She only saw that he was there waiting—unwilling to let her pass.

And then Bree knew. *Mikkel saved me from stepping off into nothing.*

Unable to speak, Bree stared at him. Tears blurred her sight. No matter how much she wanted to hide her feelings, she could not.

A shadow passed over Mikkel's face. Even in the strange light, Bree could see the expression in his eyes. For an instant she wondered if he, having found her, truly wanted to take her back. Then she decided that she was hoping for too much.

Just the same, Mikkel swallowed before speaking. He cleared his throat, then asked, "Do I need to tie your hands?"

Unable to speak, Bree shook her head.

Mikkel's face hardened. "Where are my silver coins?"

"Your coins?" Right now, Mikkel's missing coins were the furthest thing from Bree's mind. At least Mikkel wasn't reminding her that he saved her life.

"What did you do with them?" he asked.

"I don't have your coins."

"You took them from the ship the night you disappeared."

"No, I didn't. I've never even seen your bag of coins."

"Who else would take them? We searched the other prisoners and all their belongings."

Bree sighed. How could she convince Mikkel that she was not guilty? Bree had no idea. Instead she said, "Lil has been very sick. I need to get back to her. I need to get wood."

Then Bree remembered. Getting wood no longer mattered.

As they started walking, Bree discovered that in the fog she had become completely turned around. When they reached the shelter, Lil was awake. Snuggled deep beneath her blanket, she looked up at Bree with a glad light in her eyes.

"I'm better," she said. "I'm almost well!"

In the next moment Mikkel stepped close, and Lil started to cry. Bree took the younger girl in her arms, but Lil could not stop sobbing. Finally she drew a long shuddering breath.

"Oh, Bree, it's all my fault! If I hadn't gotten sick, you would have escaped." Lil could not be comforted.

Bree looked up at Mikkel. "Please," she said. "Just go away. Pretend you never found us."

"No." He spit out the word.

"Sail on home. Leave us behind."

"No," Mikkel said again.

"We can stay here until Lil is well enough to walk. No one would find out."

"No," Mikkel said a third time. "My mother needs a slave. That slave is you."

His eyes were hard now and his face cold.

"Lil is too weak to walk," she told him.

"We'll carry her. And you'll show me where you hid my coins."

Mikkel searched out two long poles and used them to turn Lil's blanket into a stretcher. Then he and Bree helped Lil down the steep slope outside the shelter.

By the time they were ready to leave, the fog had become a thin mist. With Mikkel at the front end and Bree at the back, they carried Lil between them.

Often Bree looked down, watching Lil's face. More than once, the eight-year-old drew long shuddering breaths and started crying again.

We came so close, Bree thought. *But we didn't win.* Worst of all, this wasn't just a contest, like a race Dev ran against his friends. This counted for life, and they had lost.

With every step, Bree tried to push away one thought. *Lil's right. If I hadn't brought her along, I would have escaped.* Every time Bree thought about it, she felt more upset.

But then as they walked, Bree glanced down at Lil. The eight-year-old had pushed aside her blanket just enough for Bree to see. She lay with her arms crossed over her chest.

"Courage to win," Lil whispered when Bree set the stretcher down.

"Courage to win, Lil," Bree whispered back. "Jesus is Savior, Lord, and King."

"And Friend." For the first time since Mikkel found the girls, Lil's eyes shone with faith.

For the first time since Mikkel appeared, Bree thought of one good thing about going back to the ship. She would see her friend Nola, the kind Irish woman, again.

Mikkel took a different route than the one by which Bree and Lil had come. When the side of the mountain became too steep to use the stretcher, he set it on the ground and knelt down next to Lil.

"I have to carry you," he explained, and Bree felt surprised at the kindness in his voice. "I have to put you over my shoulder so I have one hand free. But I'll do my best to take good care of you."

As Mikkel lifted Lil, Bree saw his eyes. If she didn't know better, she would think he was sorry for what had happened to Lil. Once before, Bree had glimpsed Mikkel's kindness. Whenever it showed, he quickly covered it up. Maybe his heart wasn't as hard as Bree thought. Could Mikkel possibly understand what he'd done to all the Irish he had captured?

On their way back to the ship, Mikkel stopped at the hollow in the rocks where Bree and Lil had hidden. From there he led them to the stream, and then the fire ring.

"You found each of these places?" Bree felt surprised. "You knew where we were?"

"I knew what you needed. I looked for water and a place to build a fire. But I never found your footprints. Just big ones—the size of a man's foot."

At each place he asked, "Where did you hide the coins?"

Each time she told him, "I haven't seen your bag of coins." And now she had her own questions. "So why don't you tell me something? Did you earn the coins in trade?"

"Not exactly."

Bree stared at him. "Not exactly?"

"Inside the big bag are three smaller ones. I earned some of the coins and some I collected."

Bree thought she knew what that meant. "And I get blamed for stealing your horde of coins. The coins you stole in the first place?"

A wide grin lit Mikkel's windburned face. "It looks that way. So be a good lass and get them for me."

Bree couldn't believe what she was hearing. "You understand, don't you, that I have a conscience about something like this? How can you expect me to help you find something you stole from the Irish?"

Mikkel's grin faded. "You don't have any choice. Everyone believes that you're guilty. If you value your life, you'll give me the coins."

A hard knot tightened Bree's stomach. The prideful

young man had returned. Mikkel's kindness toward Lil already seemed a far-off dream.

"All right," Bree said slowly. "The last night I was here I saw something, but I don't know what it was or what it meant."

Bree led Mikkel down the mountainside to the large rock she remembered as a marker. When she dug beneath fallen leaves, she found no stick, but the small rock lay nearby.

Bree put it in place, took one of the poles from Lil's stretcher, and set that in place also. "I'm not strong enough to lift the rock," she said.

"Try," Mikkel answered.

Leaning her entire weight into it, Bree pushed down on the stick. The large rock didn't move even an inch. When Mikkel took his turn, it lifted easily.

"Let's see if there's a hollow underneath," Bree said. "It might hold your coins."

There was a hollow, all right, but it was empty. Whatever had been there was gone.

"So these are the coins you're talking about?" Mikkel scoffed.

Bree stepped back. "I told you. I didn't take them."

"But you did see the bag of coins, after all?"

Bree shook her head. "All I saw was a silhouette. A dark shape against the gray light outside the trees."

"Where did you put the coins next?"

Filled with anger, Bree could barely speak. "Don't you believe a word I say?"

But then she understood. Even if she found the coins and turned them over to Mikkel, it would seem she had stolen them. No matter what she did, she would appear guilty.

Like a bird huddled in a nest of blankets, Lil lay on the stretcher with her eyes closed. Just looking at her, Bree wanted to cry. What was ahead for both of them, if Bree couldn't prove she was innocent?

Once more she made an attempt. "You searched all the Irish. Have you searched the Vikings?"

"You would accuse my own men? They're my neighbors, my relatives, my friends. We don't steal from each other."

"You don't?"

"Of course not. It's against our laws. I've known most of the men all my life."

"All of you come from the same part of Norway?"

Mikkel thought for a moment. "Not Gunnar. He's new to our fjord." Mikkel spoke slowly as if he, too, had wondered if Gunnar was guilty. "From the first he believed you stole the coins."

More than once Bree had felt uneasy about the cruel light in Gunnar's eyes. Now her anxious thoughts seemed overwhelming. *Is Gunnar the real thief? Is he trying to put the blame on me?*

SIXTEEN

THE FOREVER CHOICE

From where Bree stood next to the large rock she could see Mikkel's ship. It was still a steep walk down. Mikkel lifted Lil to his shoulder while Bree carried the poles and bundles.

The next time they stopped she asked, "Mikkel, how did you find us?"

"I prayed."

Bree stared at him. "You *prayed?*" She couldn't believe it.

"I knew I had to find you. You know your mountains, but not ours."

"But who did you pray to?"

"To my gods first. I didn't get an answer. Then I tried your God."

"You prayed to *my* God?"

Mikkel grinned. "He seems to care about you."

Bree backed away. She didn't like the idea of God helping her enemy. Whose side was He on?

"I don't understand."

"I searched everywhere. I thought maybe my gods didn't like having you here. When I tried your God, He showed me who you were."

"And that's how you found me?"

"I started looking in a different way. I told Him you needed help."

Of all the things Mikkel could have said, that upset Bree the most. "My God answered your prayer, even though you don't believe in Him?"

"Yup." Mikkel was proud of himself now. "He did the right thing, don't you think? You needed help."

But Bree felt betrayed. Betrayed and angry. As they started walking again, she cried out to God. *How can You give me away to my enemy? You're supposed to be* my *God!*

I'm Mikkel's God too.

You are? Bree asked.

He just doesn't know it yet.

Suddenly Bree snickered. Then she laughed out loud.

Mikkel turned around. "Something funny?" he asked, as if she had lost her mind.

Bree nodded.

"Why don't you tell me?"

Bree shook her head. "You wouldn't understand." To

her great embarrassment tears filled her eyes.

Seeming just as embarrassed, Mikkel faced forward and started walking again.

With each step Bree felt more upset about returning to the ship. So close she and Lil had come. So close to getting away! How could God take her and Lil that far, then let them be caught? Even help Mikkel catch them?

God, she cried out. *How can You do this to Lil and me?*

Like a wheel going round and round, Bree could think of only one thing. God hadn't answered her prayers the way she wanted. Even worse, she now wondered if He had really spoken to her on the mountain.

Deep inside Bree a sobbing began. Never in her whole life had she been so angry. Never had she been so desperate. From the bottom of her heart, she offered one more prayer. *If You're really there—if You really care about me—if You really called me to be a light to the nations, will You tell me through someone else?*

When the ground leveled off, Mikkel lowered Lil to the stretcher again. As they walked out of the trees near the Viking houses, Bree looked ahead. Mikkel's ship, the *Sea Bird,* was drawn up on shore. Nearby were the tents the Vikings had set up while she was gone. A short distance away, men, women, and children sat around the fire, eating their evening meal.

Bree's stomach rumbled with hunger. Just then a man at the fire turned, looked toward Mikkel, and spoke to the others. From one person to the next, the word passed.

In an open space Mikkel set down the stretcher. As he walked over to the fire, Vikings gathered around him, asking questions. Concerned Irish prisoners gathered around Bree.

"Lil is weak," Bree said quickly. "She's been very sick. Please help me take care of her."

Then Mikkel turned, facing Bree. In the breeze off the sea his thatch of blond hair looked as windblown as always. The kindness he had shown Lil seemed like something that never happened.

Bree straightened, lifting her chin. As though her brother Dev stood beside her, she remembered his words. "Courage to win, Bree. Courage to win." She needed that courage now. Across the distance between them, Bree's gaze met Mikkel's, and she did not blink.

Mikkel waited until everyone was silent. When he spoke, his words were cold and hard, as though he flung them into the wind. "Bree says she does not have my silver coins."

A mutter passed between the Vikings. Bree guessed what they were thinking. Who, other than Bree, could the thief be?

As angry eyes turned her way, Bree felt a hot flush of embarrassment rise to her face. Never before had she been accused of wrongdoing. As the daughter of an Irish chieftain, she had always been viewed with respect.

But now Mikkel spoke directly to the Irish. "The person who stole my coins has dishonored me. If the *ting*, the council of our freemen, believes that compensation cannot be paid, the penalty is death."

This time an angry mutter passed between the Irish. Dirty, unkempt, and still wearing the old man's clothes, Bree held her head high and would not flinch. Mikkel the raider worried about his good name? The good name of the O'Tooles had always been held in honor.

Then Lil moved. Pushing aside her blanket, she stood up. When she stumbled, Bree guessed how weak she must feel. Just the same, Lil walked over to Bree and stood next to her.

Reaching out, Bree put her arm around the younger girl's shoulders. As Lil crossed her arms over her chest, Bree felt sure of one thing. Whatever happened to Lil in the years ahead, she would be all right.

Then the Irish woman Nola stood on Bree's other side. In the next moment Bree felt movement around them. An Irishman stood to Nola's right, another on Lil's left. Men, women, and children lined up behind Bree.

For one instant Bree turned and saw their faces. *The fighting Irish,* she thought and almost smiled. *Not one of them is going to back down.*

Mikkel's eyes were hard now. His face looked much older than his years. "We will find the truth of this matter. We will also find the coins."

As though she could see it, Bree felt the anger around her. The Vikings blamed her for the theft. The Irish believed in her innocence. Standing between the two groups, Bree already felt condemned to die.

"We won't leave until you find the coins," Mikkel told the Vikings. "If you want to go home, you'd better look in some new places."

The Irish looked relieved, and Bree guessed their thoughts. They still hoped to escape. But the Vikings scowled. Another angry mutter passed between them. No doubt about it; they wanted to go home.

Though she could see no visible lines, Bree felt the sides being drawn. The battle of belief about who was guilty had only begun.

As darkness fell, the Vikings went back to the fire and the Irish returned to the ship. One of the Irishmen looked at Bree's clothes and grinned. "You're fit to lead a rebellion, you are."

Other prisoners pulled out hidden-away flatbread and cheese. "We thought you'd escape," many of them said. "We hoped that you would."

It was her friend Nola who told Bree, "Last night I had a dream. In my dream I saw Mikkel bring you back. When I started to cry, I felt a hand upon my shoulder. I turned around but could see no one. Deep inside, I sensed a quiet message—'Bree will be My servant in the lands of the North.' And I felt comforted."

Nola's hug was strong and warm. When she stood back, Nola looked into Bree's eyes. "The Lord wouldn't tell only me. You must know that too."

As Bree looked up into her friend's face, she saw truth

there. But Bree's wounded heart stood between truth and comfort. She could only say, "Thank you, Nola." And then Bree fell silent.

The rain started as a light mist but soon turned cold. Before long, the raindrops felt like needles driven against Bree's skin. She dreaded what the cold, damp weather could do to Lil.

"Please," she asked the other Irish, "can we get Lil as far under the sail as possible?" Immediately they made room for Lil in the most sheltered place they could find.

Looking down on her young friend, Bree again felt the terror she had known on the mountain. That terror was not just for herself; it was also for Lil. One thing Bree could not forget: If she had fallen from the rocks, Lil would have been left on the mountain alone.

As the rain kept on into the second day, the Irish huddled under the sail. Spread across three supports at the center of the ship, the sail hung like a tent over the sides. The Vikings stayed in their tents on shore. Everyone looked cold and miserable.

Bree's misery went even further. Angry at God, angry at being forced by rain to stay in one spot, Bree felt she was already in jail. *How can I figure out who really has the coins? How can I find a way to clear my name?*

But there was something even worse. Bree felt betrayed by the God she had trusted. *How can you answer Mikkel's prayer and not mine?* she cried out in her thoughts.

Mikkel doesn't even believe in you!

When the rain stopped for a short time, Bree took out the soapstone pot and filled it with water. It would help Lil to have something warm to drink.

A number of people stood around the fire. Among them was Gunnar. Bree glanced his way, then moved to the other side of the fire. From there she could watch him.

A scruffy beard filled Gunnar's thin face and reached up into the hollows of his cheeks. Long and lean, he always seemed to slink about. But the cruel light in his eyes bothered Bree most.

As she stood there, waiting for her water to heat, another Viking spoke to Bree. "Please," he said. "I see that you have my soapstone pot. May I have it back?"

Bree turned to him. The man's solid body was strong and muscular. Yet, in spite of weeks in the sun and wind, the skin of his face looked soft.

The man was shorter than the other Vikings. When he pushed back his knitted cap, wisps of light brown hair popped out around his ears. His voice sounded familiar, but Bree couldn't place it.

"Your pot?" she asked. "How do you know that it's yours?"

"The fasteners," he said. "See how it's cracked? I mended it myself. The fasteners hold it together."

"I'm sorry," Bree said. "We found your pot on the mountain. We didn't know it was yours."

"I left it there when I searched for you. But I always knew you were innocent."

Oh, yes, Bree thought. *Left it as bait? A trap to tell him whether we hid nearby?* Bree had wondered about that very thing.

Now she remembered where she heard his voice. While she fished, this man and Gunnar had stood behind her talking. Named Alf, he was one of the four guards.

"Thank you," Bree said. "I'm glad you believe that I'm innocent. Do you still think the trolls took the coins?"

As though the giants were listening, Alf rolled his eyes from one side to the other. Glancing around, he looked up at the trees, as if expecting the trolls to appear above them. "They're very rich, you know. Trolls store their silver and gold in the mountains."

Without saying another word, Bree emptied the soapstone pot and handed it to Alf.

As she walked away, Bree realized she had never thought about why a thief did what he did. Certainly a thief could become a wealthy man. For that to happen, he had to figure out a way to not be caught. And that required the most planning of all.

If someone wanted to steal something, what would be the best way to hide what he was doing? To put the blame on someone who had disappeared and might never be found? Or to put the blame someplace where it couldn't be proved at all?

For yet another day the rain slashed down on the harbor

between the seven mountains. Bree decided the sky was as sorry as she was about all that had happened. But something else was worse. The desperate ache in her empty heart.

For Bree the three days and three nights had been the longest in her entire life. Filled with anger, she still felt betrayed by the God she had trusted. In the long days and longer nights she had turned her back on Him. He seemed to have disappeared forever.

Inside, Bree still felt the knot of misery that had formed inside her heart when Mikkel appeared on the mountain. More than once, she had needed to forgive him. But now it was God who upset Bree most.

You promised me, Bree told Him when she woke on the third night. Slipping out from under the sail, she made her way to the bow of the ship. *Remember what You said? You promised You would never leave or forsake me. But You've gone to some far-off place. Where are You?*

Grateful that she could be alone, Bree looked off to the western islands. *Why did You betray me?* she cried out in her thoughts. *I'm Your child, and I asked You for something really important. I thought You'd help me escape.*

Standing there, Bree waited, but no answer came. Everything seemed mixed up. How could she be a light to the nations if she was only a slave?

Then as Bree looked up at the sky, the clouds moved on. The thin line of the moon shone bright. Like a whisper on the night wind Bree heard the words.

Do you also want to go away?

"Away from You?" Bree was startled. She was angry enough to do just that. "Away from You because I didn't get what I wanted?"

Then she remembered. Long ago, Jesus had taught those who followed Him something that was difficult to accept. When they deserted Him, Jesus turned to His twelve disciples and asked, "Do you also want to go away?" The book of John, chapter six, gave Peter's answer. "Lord, to whom shall we go?"

Deep in her heart Bree faced a choice that would count forever. If she turned away from the Lord now, she might never come back. But if she asked for His help, He would be with her in whatever she faced.

For the first time in days, Bree did not run away. Instead, she turned Peter's words into a prayer. *Lord, to whom shall I go? You have the words of eternal life. I have come to believe and know that You are the Christ, the Son of the living God.*

In the stillness of the night Bree sensed God's peace. And then she knew. *I want to go home to Ireland but I must learn to live here.*

For a long time she stood there thinking. God had called her to be a light to the nations. That's what she wanted to be—not because she could do it herself, but because God had promised to never leave or forsake her.

Now there was something else that Bree needed to know. *How can I make the best of what is happening to me?*

SEVENTEEN

DEVIN'S GIFT

In the morning Bjorn the cobbler brought Devin and Jeremy back to his shop. During the night he had slipped away and made new shoes for both of them. When they offered to work to pay for them, Bjorn said, "No, no, I know your father, Devin. You must get home and tell him you are restored to him. And this I will do."

The kind eyes of the cobbler met Devin's gaze. "You want to free your sister?"

Devin nodded, hardly daring to believe it would be possible.

"You want to go to Norway? You are willing to work your way?"

Again Devin nodded.

"I thought so. I'll find you passage on the ship of a man I trust. But you have to bring ransom money with you."

"How much?" Devin asked.

When Bjorn told him, Devin knew it was a staggering amount. "My sister Bree is worth all that?"

Bjorn smiled. "The Vikings think so. But something else I will do. If you can persuade Mikkel to return my coins, I will give you a reward."

When it was time to leave, Devin put on his old shoes. The jagged hole on the right sole had grown so large that he wondered how he had worn it so long. With his new shoes, a large piece of cheese, and loaves of Irish bread, Devin was ready to go.

As he and Jeremy said good-bye to Bjorn, tears again came to Devin's eyes. "I hope I never forget how you helped me forgive," he said.

"Come back when you have the ransom money," Bjorn answered. "The safe passage to Norway is my gift to your family."

When Devin left the cobbler's shop, he held his head high. Wearing his old shoes—the right shoe with its jagged tear—he set out.

For some time he and Jeremy walked up and down the streets of Dublin. Devin especially walked on the side streets where fewer footprints would trample his own. And then he walked to a gate on the side of the city.

From there he made his way down to the soft riverbank and waded into the water.

As Jeremy watched from a distance, Devin waded upstream. When he came to a large flat rock, he climbed out. There he took off his old ragged shoe.

For a moment Devin stood on the rock, looking down into the water. The river Liffey looked dark but strangely clear with the morning sun reflecting in it. As the water flowed to the sea, Devin stared down into the current and thought of home.

The only gift he could bring his family was himself. That would help, Devin knew, but it wasn't enough. It wasn't enough for him, and it wouldn't be enough for his family.

But now Devin had hope—the hope of finding Bree and bringing her home.

As he stepped off the rock, Devin wore his new shoes—shoes that made footprints that wouldn't be nearly as interesting to a man who might follow him to the Wicklow Mountains.

When Jeremy joined him, the painful knot was gone from Devin's heart. The hard sound had left his voice. "Let's go home," he said.

The next day Devin and Jeremy came to the Sugar Loaf Mountains. Farther on, they said good-bye and went two different ways. For both Devin and Jeremy the separation was hard. They had become what Devin knew would be lifelong friends.

With each step closer to home Devin grew more excited. *Mam,* he thought first. He could still see her face as they gathered around the table on Bree's birthday. Their friend, Brother Cronan, had said, "We need to keep teaching the children to trust the Lord. Let's especially encourage Briana."

"Especially?" Mam had asked, a frightened look in her eyes.

And Dad—big, strong Dad whose love surrounded them all.

His little sisters, Cara and Jen. And seven-year-old Adam. Devin had told Adam that if he managed to take care of the two little girls, he could someday be a great Irish chieftain.

The evening was soft with the mists of Ireland when Devin opened the gate in the stone fence near his home. There, to his surprise, Devin saw his mother sitting down, though it was still day. On a bench under a tree she sat with no work in hand.

For an instant Devin stood still to study his mother's face. Something was different about her. What was it?

Then out of his own newfound peace Devin knew. Suddenly he broke into a run. When his mother saw him, she leaped up from her bench. Her arms went around Devin as though she would never let him go.

When at last she stepped back, she only said, "Bree?"

"She has gone to Norway," Devin said. "I know where. She will be all right until I fetch her home."

When Devin looked into her eyes, his mam blinked her tears away. "I will always have times when I'm afraid for Bree. But God gives me His peace," she said.

Then all at once three children leaped upon Devin. When they knocked him to the ground, he and Adam rolled in the dirt. Then Adam started to cry when he realized Bree hadn't come home.

But in that moment their father was there. When his dad wrapped his arms around him, Devin felt like a young boy again. As he told how Bree bargained to set him free, Aidan O'Toole began weeping.

But then Devin said, "Someday Bree will come home again." His voice held a sureness that helped even Devin believe his own good words could be true.

Adam looked up into his eyes. "Dev, are you still my brother, even though you act different?"

Not quite sure what Adam meant, Devin only grinned. But his father said, "Devin has changed, hasn't he?"

Reaching out, Aidan O'Toole gathered all of them into his arms. "He is still your brother," he told Adam. "But Devin is grown-up now."

EIGHTEEN

THE AURLAND FJORD

At breakfast the next morning Bree decided it was time to start her new life. "I need to go back up the mountain," she told Mikkel when she found him near the fire. "And I can't go without you."

"That's for sure, you can't. You're not getting out of my sight."

"I've stayed around for three days," Bree told him. "I thought you'd trust me now."

"I do," Mikkel answered as though lying through his teeth. "I trust you if I see you."

As they started up the mountain, Mikkel set off at a pace that left Bree breathless. She could only feel glad for the many years she had climbed Brockagh, the mountain behind her home in Ireland.

"What's this all about?" Mikkel asked.

"I'm going to clear my good name. You think I can take you to the coins because I'm guilty. But if I find the coins for you, you'll still think I'm guilty. So I'll help the thief find them for you."

When they reached the big rock on the side of the mountain, Bree pointed to a spot and said, "Stand there."

Backing away, she looked at the light between the trees, then asked Mikkel to move closer to the rock. "Now, stay there. I need to climb up to the fire ring."

Mikkel gave her a long searching look. "Are you planning to disappear again?"

Bree smiled. "Well, catch me if you can!"

"Bree, I mean it."

"I mean it too. I said I'd clear my name, and I will."

"You give me your word that you won't run?"

"I give you my word. My word is good."

"I know."

"You do?" Bree asked. "You really trust me?"

"It depends. If you don't give me your word, I don't trust you. You'll escape again. But if you give me your word, I do trust you."

"Why?"

Mikkel looked away. At first Bree thought he wouldn't answer. Then he met her gaze. "Because I respect you."

When tears welled up in Bree's eyes, it surprised her. Then she felt embarrassed. Quickly she turned away. Hoping that Mikkel hadn't noticed how she felt, Bree started climbing again.

One thought pounded at her heart. She wished she could respect Mikkel, but she couldn't. She probably never would.

At the fire ring farther up the mountain, Bree stood on one side, then the other. Neither place seemed right. Standing there, Bree wondered about it. Then she remembered.

When she had seen the silhouette of someone near the big rock, she had just finished making her footprints larger. She had worked her way around the fire ring, then walked off until she reached a path. Now she found that place and looked again.

Ahhh, there she had it—a straight view down the side of the mountain and Mikkel standing next to the rock. Without letting her out of his sight, he stood there, as straight as a stick. Bree locked into her mind what she needed to know.

On the way back down the mountain, Bree said, "Tomorrow I will give you your coins. And I'll prove that I didn't take them."

"So how are you going to do all that?"

"You've spent all this time looking for me, instead of the coins."

"True."

"You thought it would be one and the same," Bree said.

Mikkel nodded. "Then for a while I forgot about the coins. Kind of strange, isn't it?"

Bree ignored his question. "You told everyone you won't leave for Aurland until you have the coins."

"The thief probably keeps moving them around." Mikkel looked at the mountains rising above the harbor. "With these mountains, and rocks, and trees we could look forever and not find them."

"The Viking who stole your coins will want to take them with him."

Suddenly Mikkel laughed. His eyes lit with excitement. "So tomorrow morning I tell everyone that we're sailing in the afternoon. I watch to see who leaves. I follow and catch the thief in the act."

Bree smiled and Mikkel laughed again. "You know, Bree, for an Irish lass you're really pretty smart."

But the next morning so many Vikings left the ship that Mikkel couldn't possibly follow all of them.

I missed it, Bree thought. *And I can't tell Mikkel where I believe the coins are. He'll still think I'm guilty.* Then she remembered her backup plan.

By midafternoon, when all the Vikings returned, a warm wind blew from the southwest. For the first time in days the sun sparkled upon blue water. Mikkel told the Irish to take down the tents.

Since their capture, the prisoners had been expected to carry a heavy part in the work. Now Mikkel ordered every prisoner except Bree off the ship. He wanted only Vikings to load the *Sea Bird.*

As he tied Bree's hands and feet, he spoke quietly. "Remember, I don't want to search all my relatives."

"You won't have to," Bree told him. "Make sure they work hard, and you will only need to search the guilty person."

From where Bree sat at the bow she looked down the length of the boat. While waiting, she remembered carrying two loaves of bread under her cloak. On her climb up the mountain they had shifted at least a hundred times.

One by one, the men brought their loads up the ramp. First came the supports for the beds and tents. Next came barrels of water and dried fish. Then each Viking set his own sea chest in place.

Most of the men worked quickly, and Gunnar was among them. Each time he glanced toward Bree, she felt dread. Still, she watched every movement of the men who worked in front of her.

In spite of his muscular build, Alf seemed to tire more quickly than the others. As with most of the Vikings he wore a tunic—a loose-fitting garment without sleeves. When he bent over to set down a cask of water, the cloth of his tunic shifted. With one swift movement

Alf touched his chest and pushed something in place. When he straightened, the cloth was smooth again.

When the *Sea Bird* was loaded, Mikkel stopped next to Bree. "It's Alf," she said quietly. But when she saw Alf looking their way, Bree cringed. *I have a new enemy,* she thought.

Mikkel stalked over to where Alf sat on his sea chest. "Get up," Mikkel ordered.

As he stood before Mikkel, Alf wore his usual smile. But then Mikkel patted his waist. In the next moment something slid down inside Alf's pant leg. It clunked on the deck.

Mikkel picked up the small bag and set it on his sea chest. As he patted Alf's chest, something else clinked. "Take off your tunic," Mikkel ordered.

Two flattened-out bags showed through the thin shirt underneath. Each bag was tied at the top with a narrow leather strip. A longer strip between them hung over the back of Alf's neck. Mikkel calmly collected his bags of silver coins.

"It's the trolls," Alf said. As though still looking for them, his eyes shifted from one side to the other. "The trolls asked me to take care of their silver."

But Mikkel ignored him. "Tie Alf up!" he ordered another Viking.

To Alf, Mikkel said, "We'll take you to Aurland. Next time the council of freemen meet, they'll decide your punishment." Alf glared at Bree, his eyes filled with hate.

When the rest of the longship was loaded, the Irish gathered once more around Bree. "Ah, lass, you have the wisdom of the Irish," one of the men said.

"God bless you, lass," said another.

Warmed by their encouragement, Bree drew a deep breath of relief. Now all she had to do was get her hands and feet set free.

But then Bree glanced toward Alf. No longer did his smiling eyes warm her heart. In spite of his tied hands and feet, Bree would stay as far from him as possible.

As they left the cluster of houses and the harbor of the seven mountains, the *Sea Bird* turned north. Soon they passed through a narrow waterway. On either side of them, rocky ledges lined the channel. Squawking gulls flew low over the ship.

When they sailed in the shelter of the land, the wind died down, and Vikings took up their oars. By the time they passed into the Sogne Fjord, the red sun rested on the waves in the west. As the *Sea Bird* turned east, the stretch of water grew wide, and the large square sail billowed in the wind.

Mikkel stood before Bree. "Your word to not jump over?" Mikkel knew she was a strong swimmer.

"My word," Bree answered.

As Mikkel untied her hands and feet, she breathed

deep, taking in the scent of the sea. But then she looked up to see Alf watching her. When she saw the anger in his eyes, a cold chill went down her spine.

Then Bree remembered standing with Alf beside the fire. He had hidden away a treasure—a bag of silver coins—yet he wanted to hang on to one broken pot. In the moment he asked for it, Bree knew he had been on the mountain. She looked at his build and guessed what his silhouette would be.

One broken pot gave him away. How could Alf be so unwise? It didn't make sense.

But then it struck Bree. *I'm a broken pot too.*

She had prayed and didn't get what she wanted. For the longest three days of her life, she hung on to her anger and pushed God away.

In that moment Bree knew she might have walked away from Him forever. Instead, she could only feel glad that He had come to her again with the treasure of His love.

Soon Bree began to understand what Mikkel meant when he talked about a fjord. A long, narrow body of water, the fjord stretched in from the sea. For much of the way, steep, rocky slopes rose straight up from the water. Here and there, narrow strips of land gave enough space for buildings and small farms.

By the time the moon came up, the ship had grown quiet. Around Bree the Irish lay sleeping. Alert Vikings stood watch, but others slept. Wanting to see everything around her, Bree struggled to stay awake. Then she, too, drifted off to sleep.

When Bree woke in the morning, a thick mist hid the mountaintops. Before long, a golden light broke through, pushing the clouds away and creating a path across the water.

Bree stood at the side of the ship, quenching her thirst for seeing what lay beyond the Irish Sea. After the days and nights of rain, she welcomed the blue skies and the sunlight on the water of the fjord.

By midafternoon Mikkel stood at the bow of his ship. Straight and strong he stood, with his blond hair blowing in the wind. As Bree watched, he glanced up at the large dragon head that rose far above him.

Bree shivered and looked away. She had never liked that snarling mouth and warlike head. The fierce dragon seemed to lead them across the water.

Then Mikkel turned and saw her there. "Come here," he invited. "I want you to see something." To Bree's surprise he spoke like a friend, instead of the master of a ship.

By now the fjord had narrowed. On either side, rock walls rose straight up from the deep blue water. Far above, waterfalls spilled over the tops of mountains, dropping from ledge to ledge to the water below.

The waterfalls reminded Bree of Keely, the sister captured by Vikings years before. A year younger than Bree, Keely had been especially close to her. Often she listened to the sounds of water in the forest around their home. "It's water music," she always said.

At first Bree didn't understand. Then one day, listening to a small waterfall instead of a great thundering one, she also heard the music. Now as the ship sailed close to one side of the fjord she could hear the tumbling of water.

"See?" Mikkel spoke with pride in his voice. "Look around you! This is the Aurland Fjord."

Golden birch clung to the rocks. Sheep and goats grazed on the steep slopes, while a man loaded hay into a small boat. Over all, the sun shone, reflecting the mountains in the water.

Then Mikkel said, "Bree, I know you won't believe this, but my mother will like you. And you will like her."

He was right. Bree didn't believe it. How could she possibly like the woman she would serve as a slave?

"I mean it," Mikkel insisted. "My mother always likes someone with spirit. That's why I'm her favorite son. She'll never say so. But I am."

Bree choked, then started coughing to cover how she felt.

But Mikkel went on. "Someday I'll take long trips across the sea."

"Back to Ireland?" Bree dreaded the thought.

"Farther. Much farther. Wait and see."

Wait and see? Not if Bree could help it.

"I'll sail to places beyond where even Vikings travel." Resting his hand on the side of the ship, Mikkel ran his fingers across the wood. "My *Sea Bird* will take me to see the world."

Bree felt his pride and excitement about coming home. As the fjord grew wide, rock walls gave way to a valley. On both sides of the river that flowed through the valley were green fields and gradual slopes. Close to the Viking ship, a waterfall spilled over the straight-up-and-down mountain and plunged to the fjord below.

Bree felt the wonder of all that she saw. "It's water music!" she exclaimed. "My sister always called it water music!"

Surprise filled Mikkel's face. "You like it the way I do," he said simply. For an instant Bree wondered if she had found a new friend.

Along one side of the river a field stretched between the water and a sheer rock cliff. "That's where I live," Mikkel said, as he pointed out the buildings. "That's our farm."

Sunlight shone on the water falling from the high cliff. Then the sun shone on the blonde hair of a tall woman standing beside the fjord. Suddenly Mikkel leaned forward, seeming to forget everything else.

The moment the Viking ship touched shore, he leaped

over the side. By the time he touched ground, the woman stood before him. Mikkel straightened and tipped his head in respect.

"Mamma," he said.

"Son," she answered. A tear slid down her cheek. "You were gone so long. I was afraid."

"I know. But I am here." Relief filled Mikkel's voice. "I am home."

Then Bree forgot everything else. As Vikings set down the ramp, people jostled around her. Bree looked into the crowd gathered to meet the ship. There Bree saw a slender girl with sandy-colored hair, brown eyes, and a dusting of freckles across her nose.

Who is she? Bree wondered. *Why do I think she's someone I know?*

The girl looked too thin, as if she had been sick. Yet she had to be at least eleven, perhaps twelve.

In the crowd of people pouring off the ship, Bree lost sight of her. Then far up on shore, Bree saw her again. Could it possibly be?

It's my sister Keely!

Across the distance their gazes met. The girl's mouth formed a round O, a gasp of recognition. Then suddenly she turned away.

A tall Viking stood in front of Bree, blocking her view. Frantically Bree tried to get around him. By the time she reached the side of the ship, the girl was gone.

It was Keely, Bree thought. *I know it was Keely!*

But if it was, why did she turn away? Why did she act as if she didn't know me?

I'll find her, Bree promised herself. *I'll find my sister!*

ACKNOWLEDGMENTS

In a long-ago story called a saga, a man named Brynjulf was a wise and good father. When his son wanted to go a-viking, Brynjulf refused to give him a warship. Instead, Brynjulf equipped him with a merchant ship and crew, saying, "I want you to be a merchant—a trader of furs and other goods. And when you go, take the south route. Go to Dublin, for that is the voyage I like best."

From the beginning of time there have been people who take what seems to be the easy way out. But there have also been those who choose to live with courage. Such a man was Brynjulf, a chieftain of high rank who lived in Aurland, Norway, and talked with his son just before the year 900. And such a man is Anders Ohnstad.

Historian, author, and retired high school teacher, Anders helped me with his articles and books, his warm Norwegian welcome, his thoughtful, in-depth knowledge, and his personal faith and courage. Thank you, Anders, for the long talks in which you made the history of the Aurland area come alive. Thank you for the insights that helped me understand who Mikkel and his father should be.

My gratitude also to Åsmund Ohnstad, editor of *Among the Fjords and Mountains: A Summary of Aurland's History,* (Aurland Historical Association, 1994), and all the authors of this excellent book. Thanks, Svein Indrelid, for recounting the story of Brynjulf.

With a thankful heart I also acknowledge the help of the following:

The Local History Center in Aurland and each person who patiently answered my questions: Ingvar Vikesland, teacher and headmaster, now principal at the center, gifted communicator, and able guide; Åsmund Ohnstad, high school teacher, author, and editor; Frazier LaForce, also a teacher and local cultural consultant.

Al and Iva Danielson, who first told me about Aurland; Ester Vikesland who helped me while I was there; Dr. Arne Brekke, president, Brekke Tours and Travel, and former professor of Germanic languages, University of North Dakota, Grand Forks; Millie Ohnstad, heritage tour leader and genealogical editor of *Aurland Newsletter, Past and Present.* My gratitude, Millie, for your enthusiasm, photos, and practical help.

The Viking Ship Museum, Oslo; the Bergen Maritime Museum, Bergen; and Captain Bjørn Ols'en, retired, volunteer, for his helpful explanations.

Janicke Larsen, educational officer, Bergen Maritime Museum, Bergen. Thanks, Janicke, not only for answering questions, but also for searching out countless details. In both Bergen and the Glendalough Monastery area in Ireland the kind of trees on the mountains have changed since Viking times.

Dr. Bjorn Hurlen, Lake Region Family Chiropractic Clinic, Alexandria, Minnesota, and a former resident of Bergen. Thanks, Bjorn, for your careful reading of both this manuscript and the first novel in the series. I value your great suggestions, your encouragement, and your careful attention to detail.

The Sons of Norway for the resources at their Minneapolis headquarters and their *Viking* magazine; Liv Dahl, Consulate of Norway, twenty-year columnist, *Viking* magazine, and heritage programs manager, Sons of Norway; Dennis Rusinko and other members of the Viking Age Club, Chaska, Minnesota.

Vikings: The North Atlantic Saga exhibit, organized by the Smithsonian's National Museum of Natural History,

Washington, D.C., exhibited at the Science Museum of Minnesota, St. Paul.

Mary Ekola, fabric artist, for her many practical insights; Tristram Eley, senior trainer, Communicaid House, London, England, because he, like Bree, knows what it means to camp on a Bergen mountainside and live to tell about it!

Elaine Roub for her incredible hospitality, creativity, and patience in exploring all the places I wanted to see. Thanks, Elaine, for showing me the Ireland you love, for walking the mountains and seashores with me, and for reading the Irish portions of this manuscript. Your timely way of speaking into my life always amazes me!

Special resource people—David and Anne Gran, Dee and Chuck Brown, Charlotte Adelsperger, Norma Spande, my Thursday morning group, and longtime praying friends.

My agent Lee Hough and Alive Communications; Ron Klug, wise encourager and friend; Barbara LeVan Fisher for her attractive cover design and Viking logo; Greg Call for his exciting cover illustration of Bree and Mikkel and his black-and-white sketches.

My supportive editors Michele Straubel, Cessandra Dillon, and Pam Pugh; author relations manager Amy Peterson, typesetter Carolyn McDaniel, and the entire Moody team.

Finally, my deep appreciation to my husband Roy for his creative ideas, faithful encouragement, and steadfast loyalty in all the years of our marriage. Thanks for being my favorite Norwegian Viking!

Most of all, my gratitude to my Lord, who is always willing to walk ahead of me.

In addition to the Aurland book already mentioned, I have found the following books and Website especially helpful:

Delaney, Mary Murray. *Of Irish Ways.* Minneapolis: Dillon Press, 1973.

Fitzhugh, William W. and Elisabeth I. Ward, editors. *Vikings: The North Atlantic Saga.* Washington and London: Smithsonian Institution Press, in association with the National Museum of Natural History, 2000.

Haywood, John. *Encyclopaedia of the Viking Age.* New York: Thames and Hudson, Inc., 2000.

Joyce, P. W. *A Social History of Ancient Ireland,* vol. I & 2, originally published 1903, republished in the U. S., Kansas City, Mo.: Irish Genealogical Foundation, 1997.

MacManus, Seumas. *The Story of the Irish Race: A Popular History of Ireland.* New York: The Devin-Adair Co., 1921.

Sawyer, Peter, editor. *The Oxford Illustrated History of the Vikings.* Oxford, Eng: Oxford University Press, 1997.

The Viking Network Website, sponsored by the Nordic Council of Ministers, http://viking.no.

More from Lois Walfrid Johnson & Moody Publishers

Viking Quest Series

Raiders from the Sea

In one harrowing day, Viking raiders capture Bree and her brother Devin and take them from their home in Ireland. After the young Viking leader Mikkel sets Devin free on the Irish coast, Bree and Devin embark on separate journeys to courage.

ISBN: 978-0-8024-3112-7

The Invisible Friend

Bree arrives in Norway and is sent to work as a slave for the family of Mikkel, her young Viking captor. She struggles to adjust to the life of a slave, feeling worthless and disrespected, and asking God why He wants her in Norway. As God answers her prayers, Bree faces an important question: No matter who we are or where we live, what does it mean to be truly free?

ISBN: 978-0-8024-3114-1

Call 1-800-678-8812 or visit www.moodypublishers.com

Heart of Courage

In exchange for Bree's freedom, Devin and Bree have agreed to make one voyage on Mikkel's new Viking ship, Conquest. With explorer Leif Erikson they travel from Norway to Iceland, then to Greenland and beyond, encountering the dangers of the northern waters and an unknown enemy within the ship's crew.

ISBN: 978-08024-3115-8

The Raider's Promise

During her years as a captive of Mikkel, the Viking raider, Briana O'Toole has longed to return to her family and resume her life in Ireland. Yet she has changed. Bree finds herself excited to be on Leif Erikson's ship and be part of the discovery and exploration of new lands. Will Bree and Devin's knowledge of Mikkel's secret put them in danger?

ISBN: 978-0-8024-3116-5

Discover more about the author and her books at
www.lwjbooks.com.